SASQUATCH MAN

John P. Burling

Published by Wennington Press

Copyright © 2013 John P. Burling

John P. Burling has asserted his right under the Copyright, Designs and Patents Act 1988 to be identified as the author of this work.

British Library Cataloguing in Publication Data.

A catalogue record for this book is available from the British Library.

All rights reserved.

This book is sold subject to the condition that it shall not, by way of trade or otherwise, be lent, resold, hired out or otherwise circulated without the publisher's prior consent in any form of binding or cover other than that in which it is published and without a similar condition, including this condition, being imposed on the subsequent purchaser.

ISBN: 0957635907

ISBN-13: 978-0-9576359-0-6

My first born, for my first born.

CONTENTS

	Preface	1
	Prologue	4
1	Revelation	6
2	The Drifter	22
3	In Search of Eagle Feathers	42
4	The Hidden Valley	68
5	A Soldier's Pride	108
6	The Law of Anger	126
7	Seeds of Destruction	158
8	The Death of Innocence	178
9	Vengeance	202
10	Flight to Safety	217
11	The Forked Path	225
12	Pursuit	242
13	Freedom	263
14	Strange Medicine	274
15	Sasquatch Man	294

Proofread and edited by SAB Ltd.

PREFACE

The continent of North America was one of the last areas of the Earth's surface to be colonized by mankind. Anthropologists and historians have ascertained that the earliest men to live there were Stone Age hunters. It seems likely that these prehistoric wanderers followed animal tracks across an ancient land link that once connected the landmass of Asia to the unexplored territory of the Americas. At first, the ancient explorers encountered only frozen tundra and mountainous wastes; but, as they moved further south, they encountered areas favoured by a warmer climate - where they discovered strange herbs, new fruits and vast herds of buffalo, deer and bighorn sheep.

The plentiful supply of food encouraged the hunters to spread out across the plains and to eventually form small, permanent settlements belonging to particular groups. With the passage of time, the groups developed individual tribal identities and lore. In this manner, the great Native American tribes we know of today became established.

The tribes prospered for many thousands of years, untroubled by events elsewhere on the globe. It must have seemed to them that their way of life would endure for eternity. But, in fact, the peaceful idyll they had enjoyed for so long was destined to end abruptly and calamitously.

The coming of the 'white man' sounded the death knell for many tribes. Today, some are only remembered in the name of a town, city or state - and these apologetic references serve as sad memorials to a vanished culture.

The Sasquatchoni tribe was one of many to suffer the all-too-common fate of being broken up and destroyed by the advance of the second wave of European settlers. They had been notable for their genetic advantages; they were taller and stronger than the average Native American or European and had a sophisticated culture that allowed them to adapt to many changes of circumstance. But, by 1866, not a single living descendent of the once-proud Sasquatchoni people could be traced. Many academics of the period concluded that this unique tribe had effectively been exterminated.

PREFACE

Indeed, most of them had long since departed to enjoy the munificence of the Great Spirit, and to hunt with their ancestors.

But, despite everything, a few remained alive…

PROLOGUE

Slaney Driscoll, homesteader, was jolted from an undisturbed sleep to instant wakefulness. He felt suddenly threatened, but could not explain why... Was it the cold air of early dawn, or the creak of a loose floorboard? Was it the climactic terror of a nightmare, or had something moved across the light from the window?

He wrinkled his nose at the strong animal smell that pervaded the cabin and a shaft of fear hit him; his instinct told him that something feral and dangerous was nearby.

He sat bolt upright in the bed. His woman was still sleeping beside him. Reluctant to wake her, he gripped his handgun and drew back the blankets. Silently, he opened the door to the parlor.

The animal odor was overpowering. A dark shape was crouched at the far end of the room near the cold fire hob. It slavered as it tore ravenously at strips of drying meat in the larder. He could barely make out its form, but whatever it was, it was big...

Before he could collect his senses, the huge beast was upon him. As Slaney fought for his life, his fingers twined through the thick, wiry hair that covered its body. The creature was immensely strong and Slaney could not repel it, nor bring his gun to bear. He yelled as the man-like beast lifted him up and threw him with great force against the cabin wall.

As Slaney crumpled into a heap on the floor the creature twisted around and loped out through the open door.

"Slaney, is that you?"

Dazed, but recovering fast, Slaney pulled his long barrelled rifle from the wall and jerked a bullet into the breach.

"Slaney, answer me, damn you!"

The first light of dawn was just beginning to shine over the mountain range. Its rays caught the tips of the tall, yellow corncobs as they rippled and swayed in the breeze.

The creature had covered a lot of ground; it was heading for the maize plantation.

Driscoll squeezed off his first shot at two hundred yards, then another.

1. REVELATION

"Señor, you have eaten nothing!"

The angry old Mexican woman continued to mumble in Spanish as she cleared the breakfast meal from the table. "For twenty years I have slaved for you - I cook, I wash and I clean for you. Now, you refuse to eat the food!" Muttering softly to herself she pushed her way through the swing doors into the kitchen.

Swallowing the last of his coffee the big man pushed back his chair and threw his newspaper onto the table. He grinned and said: "After twenty years, Maria's still the boss!"

He looked across the table into the light brown eyes of his wife. She was in her early fifties, a beautiful, dark-haired, olive-skinned woman who, despite her years, could still attract admiring glances from male onlookers. She gave an understanding smile before replying: "Be honest with me, Timothy: you love it when she bosses you around."

REVELATION

She rose from her chair, folded her napkin neatly and placed it alongside her plate. Then she went over to her husband and stood by him. He put his arms around her waist and kissed her.

"I sometimes think she was the best part of your dowry, Condesa Isabellita Mendoza-Castillos O'Hara - phew!"

"Si, and for once you said my name correctly, hombre," she chided, smiling gently. Freeing herself, she held her husband's hand and said: "Remember, Timothy O'Hara - you are no longer a senator, you are a working rancher and old Maria likes to feed you. She cares about you."

He smiled briefly and nodded, but it was obvious that his mind was elsewhere. A distant look had entered his eyes.

Choosing her words carefully, his wife continued: "Tim - when you were reading the newspaper just now, I could see you were troubled by something. It showed on your face. You looked concerned. What's wrong? Please tell me."

Picking up the two-day old newspaper, O'Hara found the paragraph he had been reading and pointed it out to his wife.

'Mystery'

The body of a six foot six, three hundred pound Indian male was recently discovered dead in a densely wooded area of Lewistown, Dewey County, South Dakota. The man had a number of wounds on his back, which appear to have been the cause of death. The only clue as to the identity of the deceased is a gold ring found on the body. Information required by the Sheriff's Office.

'Bellita looked toward her husband; he was stroking the bristle on his chin, lost in thought. Suddenly, with an unblinking gaze, he stared up at the cavalry sword hanging above the fire grate.

"Tim," she said. There was no response. Again - "Timothy!"

Startled by the vehemence in her voice, he apologised and explained himself.

"It was twenty years back in the past - way back. The thing is, I think I know the name of that gentleman - the man they're enquiring about."

"You are sure?" asked Bellita.

"As sure as I'm sitting here looking at you, sweetheart."

"Then you must go to Lewistown."

"Yes, you're right, as usual. I won't be able to rest until I've seen the body."

'Bellita asked no more questions about the dead Indian. The set look on her husband's face said it all.

"When will you go?"

O'Hara pulled out his timepiece. "I'll catch the noon train," he said.

"Si, Timothy, we will catch the noon train!" Her words had the bite of finality. 'Bellita would brook no argument: she would not be left behind.

"Sure, why not?" smiled O'Hara.

'Bellita hurried herself, packing a valise for their overnight stay. Tim O'Hara was struggling with a problem and was sure he'd made the right decision.

Hesitantly, he unhooked a beautifully carved Indian smoking pipe from the wall above his bureau. It was patterned with unusual designs and inlaid with silver and gold. He ran his fingers over it in a soft caress.

"If only you could speak," he said wistfully. "There's many a tale you could tell."

With a mischievous look crinkling the corner of his

eyes, he called to 'Bellita.

"Señora, ready when you are. We are late!"

* * * *

"Boy! Take this gentleman's bag to room twenty-seven. If there's anything more you require, sir, please ask. The Lewistown Hotel is at your service, and we aim to…"

Before the talkative clerk could continue, O'Hara flipped the bag-boy a coin. "Where's the Sheriff's Office, son?"

"Two blocks on the right as you leave the hotel, mister."

"Thank you." Taking 'Bellita by the arm O'Hara walked out.

"Before I show you the ring," Sheriff Bishop said, "can you describe any distinctive marks that will identify it as your'n?"

"Sure can. It's gold with a flat top. And it has a shamrock with a capital letter 'T' scratched upon it."

The sheriff sucked his teeth briefly before throwing the ring to O'Hara. "It's your'n all right," he said. "Let's go and see if you can identify the dead Injun."

O'Hara and 'Bellita followed him through the

doorway and onto the sidewalk.

"This way sir," said the undertaker, stepping into a cool, low room. O'Hara began to walk forward, then stopped abruptly. He turned to Isabellita; she answered his unspoken question directly:

"I have seen death many times, Si!"

Nodding his head, O'Hara moved aside.

The undertaker pulled back the sheet. "Well, do you recognise him?" asked the sheriff. "Sure is a lot of flesh covering those bones – did ya ever see an Indian that big?"

"Madre mia!" Isabellita crossed herself and said a prayer for the soul of the dead Indian. O'Hara was silent. He stared at the impressive physique of the dead man - his friend, RoShann - for some moments before answering. Poker faced, he turned to the sheriff and shook his head.

"Nope. I'm sorry, sheriff, I don't know this man. My friend was older and not so tall."

"Well," said the sheriff, "I guess he must have traded the ring with this dead buck. I sure 'nough wouldn't have liked bumping into this big bastard on a dark night." His stiff finger prodded the body speculatively.

"Uh - begging your pardon, ma'am." The sheriff touched his hat, abashed that he had used a saloon bar expression in the presence of a lady.

"We reckon he was killed by another buck and then stripped naked," explained the sheriff. "Most often we just bury dead Indians on the spot where they've been found, but on this occasion it was a huntin' party that discovered him and a reporter was tagging along. So they brought him back here."

"Can I bury the Indian now, sheriff?" enquired the undertaker plaintively.

"Sure, why not? I…"

"No! That's for me to do!" said O'Hara forcefully. The two men stared at him, surprised at the sudden change in his tone. He glared back at them. "That is, if you have no objections?" He tossed the ring into the air as an indication of his debt. "I owe him. He died, and I got my ring back. Least I can do is bury him."

The lawman nodded his head, understanding the sentiment. "He's your'n, too," he said, simply.

O'Hara threw a hundred dollars to the surprised undertaker. "Wrap the body in some burlap for me, will yuh?"

"Yes sir, most certainly, sir. The body will be ready within the hour."

Isabellita skillfully pulled on the reins and backed the horses up until the wagon was directly beneath the branches of a large tree. "Whoa, muchachas," she called out firmly.

Resting for a moment to catch his breath, O'Hara muttered to himself: *"Goddam it! Sixty years old and I'm climbing trees!"* He looked down and saw the lifeless body of the dead Indian lying on the wagon. Snaking along the thickest branch, he looped a rope over it and threw the ends down to his wife.

"Tie one end around the body, 'Bellita, then unhitch the horses and secure the other end onto the harness."

"Are you all right, Tim?" questioned Isabellita, looking up at him.

"Yeah, I'll survive - I think," he replied sardonically. "When you're ready?"

Carefully leading the horses, she watched the body rise slowly up from the back of the wagon, high enough for O'Hara to be able to pull it over towards him. With great effort, he dragged it onto a roughly made platform he had constructed between the boughs. Breathing hard and with sweat rolling down his back, he began to lay the Indian out properly. When he was satisfied with the position of the body, O'Hara cut the burlap so that the dead man's face was exposed to the sky. Taking the smoking pipe from his belt, he placed it upon the corpse.

Done at last, he held onto a branch and carefully

lowered himself down until he was directly above the wagon. Gritting his teeth, he released his grip. For a big man he was still agile and managed to land comfortably on the balls of his feet. He walked along the wagon to sit once more beside his wife. As he settled down on the bench seat, he pulled out his kerchief and wiped his brow.

"Not bad for an old man, eh, 'Bellita?"

"You are loco, hombre, but I love you!" she smiled.

They sat looking at each other. O'Hara's face was pale and drawn. "Are you sure you have rested long enough, Tim?" queried Isabellita, her voice full of concern.

"Sure I am," said O'Hara, nodding his head. "I'm okay - just a little dizzy spell." He was grateful for a sudden draught of cold air as he glanced upward at the nearby Snow Mountain. Its sombre presence seemed to be brooding over the death of the Indian.

Their task completed, Isabellita raised her voice and shouted to the horses: "Adelante muchachas!" Leaning into their harnesses the horses began to take the strain and the wagon slowly got underway. Pulling hard on the reins, Isabellita ran them around in a U turn, putting the wagon back on the trail and taking it past the tree once more.

" Vaya usted con Dios, Amigo!" murmured Isabellita.

"*Hoka hey*, RoShann!" said O'Hara quietly. "*It's a good day to die...*"

REVELATION

As they rode back together in silence Isabellita thought about her husband's recent actions. She was brimming with curiosity - but he offered no explanation and she could sense that he wanted no questions. He seemed to be mourning something or someone. As he looked back at the receding mountains and the forest, his face registered his sadness. For the moment, he was closed to her. Only the occasional bump or lurch of the wagon kept them in contact with each other.

That night, back in the Lewistown Hotel, Isabellita found it hard to sleep. She twisted and turned, pondering the day's events: *'Who was that dead Indian? Where did he come from? Who killed him? Why did Tim tell the sheriff that he didn't recognise the dead man - when he obviously did?'*

Weary and exhausted, she fell into a fitful slumber.

Early next morning they bathed, drank their coffee and paid their bill. Saying their final goodbyes to the hotel staff, they stepped out of the main doorway onto the sidewalk. With time to spare, they decided to do a little shopping and have a meal before catching the noon train.

"I'm so pleased to be going home, Tim," said Isabellita, hugging O'Hara's arm as they took their seats. "Back to the ranch, the children and all the things that are familiar to me. There's nothing like that comfortable feeling of being where you belong."

After an hour of the journey had elapsed, the train had acquired a fair head of steam. Every mile it travelled took the swaying coaches through a subtly altered landscape. The prairie was mostly brown and windswept, though a few well-watered green grasslands appeared here and there. The flat terrain was dotted with scattered homesteads wired off from the huge cattle herds.

Isabellita thought the train seemed to go even faster whenever it approached a small town - as though it did not consider the place important enough to stop at.

Bored with looking at the scenery, she turned to her husband. "Tim, I…"

O'Hara interceded quickly, holding up his hand to silence any further comment. He knew precisely what she was going to say. Reaching into his inside pocket he pulled out an envelope containing some newspaper clippings - many of them faded and yellowed with age.

"Read those first, 'Bellita," he said, as he handed them to her. "Then we'll talk. They're the foundations of this story…" - he checked himself in mid-sentence, then said emphatically - "no, Ma'am, correction: they *are* the story!"

Glancing at the first clipping, Isabellita began to read:

REVELATION

(NEBRASKA SUN 1882)
SHERIFF'S OFFICE INVESTIGATES
REPORTS OF GIANT FOOTPRINTS

...As part of the investigation, statements were taken from local people and one of their number claimed to have seen a huge wild man who, upon being disturbed, raced off into the brushwood and escaped. During the sheriff's investigations at the ranch, cattleman Chuck Envers said: 'Old Bigfoot, he was more scared of me than I ever was of him! As soon as we set eyes on each other, that creature, why, he just took off like the wind!'

***

(MONTANA NEWS 1883)
TRAPPER REPORTS SIGHTING OF
GIANT WILD MAN

...The trapper is adamant that the creature was not a figment of his imagination, but a full-grown beast at least 7ft tall.

The witness is known to be a man of good character and sober disposition and his friends insist he would not invent such a story just to make a stir. To anyone else, however, the tale appears hardly credible.

***

(WASHINGTON TIMES 1885)

An interesting report has been received from Senator Turberville Smith, who has recently returned from a hunting trip to British Columbia, a province of Canada:

"We were moving very quietly following the tracks of bighorn sheep when, suddenly, there it was – the most amazing thing my eyes have ever witnessed. My guide and I had, purely by chance, stumbled upon a strange man-like creature as it was attempting to drink from a pool. It was just as startled as we were and all three of us stood there transfixed, frozen in our tracks. When the

creature rediscovered its senses it just hightailed it away."

The senator gave a more detailed description of the beast to our correspondent: "The creature was tall in stature and weighed around two hundred and fifty pounds — maybe more. Its body was covered in reddish brown hair. When I asked my Indian guide if he knew what it was, he replied: A Sasquatch Man!"

O'Hara was watching his wife intently. Her brow creased in concentration as her body swayed gently with the motion of the speeding train. Suddenly, her eyes opened wide, confusion and bewilderment showing on her face.

"Tim!" She shook her head, disturbed by what she had read. "I'm sorry, I do not understand!"

Rubbing a hand over his face, O'Hara came to a decision.

"Okay 'Bellita, I'll explain it all. When I've finished my story you'll understand exactly what we're doing here." He glanced over his shoulder to observe the rest of the passengers. Satisfied they were all absorbed by other matters, he continued talking. "I want you to swear for your own safety and for my peace of mind, that you will never mention this story to anyone!"

Isabellita's eyes opened wider after this dramatic announcement and she grasped her husband's hand.

"Santa Maria! On the lives of our children, Timothy, I swear!"

He stared through the window for a few moments, his eyes blind to the scenery as it flashed past, his mind struggling to rewind the passage of the years - back to the memory of the day when it first started.

"D'you remember twenty years back, when we first met - when I was Superintendent of Indian Affairs?"

Nodding her head, Isabellita smiled back. "How could I ever forget, señor?"

He acknowledged the compliment by gently squeezing her hand.

"And before that, as you know, I was a major in the army."

Taking a deep breath, he expelled the air hurriedly.

"Well, I suppose the story began the day I called on a friend of mine; his name was Jedediah Jones. He was an old trapper who ran a trading store."

Turning his head, he gazed once more through the

car window; in the far distance he could make out a flock of birds, wheeling in formation.

"Yeah, I remember. I stopped my patrol there to water our horses…"

2. THE DRIFTER

Jedediah Jones rose quickly from his bed, as fast as his arthritic limbs would allow. A groan eased its way through his tight-pinched lips as the first light of dawn framed the doorway.

Lady, his Indian wife, rubbed sleep from her eyes. "What's wrong?" she enquired.

Long acquaintance with the dangers of their home territory had impressed on both of them the need to be watchful. She knew her husband's philosophy: *'Ignore any odd sound or movement at your peril!'*

They were isolated at their trading post, but that did not concern Lady; as a grown woman she had known no other life. Her Shawnee father, with much wisdom, had bartered her for two horses and a rifle. Trapping in the far country was never easy for a white man. She had helped Jed to skin buffalo and beaver hides. Her recollections of the hard, lonely work were still fresh and green. When the trapping season came to a close and they were snowbound in their cabin she would cook the food and keep her husband warm in bed. At times she was filled with a great sadness for the loss of her babies, but the years had passed swiftly; Lady and Jed had grown old together and the shared hardships had forged a strong bond between them. She cared deeply for him.

Throwing back the fur-skinned covers of her bed, Chioe, a young Sasquatchoni girl of seventeen summers, could not contain her curiosity. "Was that gunfire?" she said.

"Yep, it was. But don't bother y'head about it!" replied Jed gruffly. He spoke to the girl as he groped above the fire mantle to lift his old Springfield rifle off its mounts. He knew full well that she would not stay in her bed; it was Jed's opinion that Indian females were amongst the most stubborn, obstinate and independent women he had ever encountered.

Chioe quickly pulled her supple buckskin dress over her body and crossed to the shuttered window. Warily, she peered through a gap in the frame.

Lady grabbed a rifle. As was the way with trappers,

Jed had trained his woman to be able to handle a weapon competently; she was a good shot.

"Watch m'back, Lady," said Jed, as he made for the door. Slipping the bar, he stepped carefully outside and listened.

Jed looked into his small corral and watched his milk cow as she wet-nursed her calf. Rubbing the cow's ear, he whispered, "Well, you sure 'nough made me a good one this time gal!"

Suddenly, a figure broke through an area of thick woodland off to the right – it was a man, running scared. As he ran, the man looked back, stopped, and fired again into the brush. Now he moved quickly, heading directly for the trading post.

Resting his rifle upon the corral post, Jed took careful aim and fired. The boom of the Springfield frightened the nearby cattle stock – they raced around and around the small corral.

The heavy bullet kicked up some dust in front of the running man, who hesitated and then ran even faster. Picking up his Remington, Jed fired off another round.

"The next bullet will be right between your eyes!" he yelled at the stranger.

This time the man came to a dead stop.

"Hold your rifle by the barrel, mister; above your head – and walk towards me slowly."

The stranger – still glancing behind – stepped tentatively forward.

"Hold it right there, mister! Now put the rifle behind your back and drop it."

As the weapon clattered to the ground, Jed jerked his Remington to the left. The stranger complied with the unspoken order and moved away from his discarded rifle.

The man eyed Jed thoughtfully before breaking the silence. In a genial tone, he said: "I like your style, old man – it shows you don't take no chances!"

Jed ignored the man's gratifying remark and examined him closely. He was not well disposed toward the stranger. The man was short, dark-haired and unshaven. His clothes were badly in need of repair and on his head he wore the battered peak cap of a Union soldier. Jed's thoughts raced, trying to size-up the man: *'Could be an army deserter, or maybe he's just one of those footloose drifters who're scattered all over this territory. Can't trust any of 'em – they'd cut your throat just to keep their knives sharp. Mean bastards – all of 'em.'*

The stranger interrupted Jed's suspicious appraisal:

"Say, mister! What kind of creatures y'all got in them woods?"

"Just the usual four-legged kind, why?"

"Well, I've just been chased away from my camp by some big, hairy, son of a bitch. Must've been all of seven feet high!"

The stranger held an arm above his head to indicate the size of his assailant.

"A bear, y'mean?" asked Jed, puzzled.

"No, sir, not on your sweet life it wasn't. A bear don't pitch rocks at a man. This thing was big and hairy like a bear, but shaped more like a man. When I loosed off my last shot at it, it seemed to know I was trying to kill it and it came charging after me. Whatever it was, it scared the shit out of me!"

The man was still shaking slightly, his nerves not yet settled. Jed looked pointedly at him, trying to decide if he should be given any credence.

Wrinkling his nose, he said: "Yep, I reckon it did. Throw some water over yourself. You can eat with us before you move on."

"I'm obliged, mister. I've heard tell of your place. You must be Jedediah Jones?"

Without waiting for a reply the stranger walked over to the water trough. He half turned before dowsing his face:

"I'm Jango, by the way!"

After cleaning himself up Jango did not look any better, or smell any sweeter, but he had at least tried to improve matters. He sat down at the table to enjoy Jed's hospitality, piling his tin plate full of food before wolfing it down ravenously. Lady, Jed's Indian wife, was refilling their cups with hot coffee. His mouth full of food, Jango commented:

"I didn't know yuh was a squawman, Jed. I'm gonna get myself one of them, one day. I…"

He cut his sentence short as Chioe, the young Sasquatchoni girl walked into the room. Her eyes glanced fleetingly at Jango as she moved past him to go through the door to the corral.

Jango's eyes locked on to the tall statuesque figure of the young Indian girl as she left the room. He couldn't believe his luck. He licked his lips lustfully, excited by the girl's heavy breasts and shapely thighs.

"Ha! Why, you sly old buck - ain't you just? You sure got yourself a real beauty there, Jed! What d'ya say I take her into the barn and give her one? I'm sure horny for her – it's been a long time, too damn long!"

Jango sat at the table shaking his head disconsolately, his fingers drumming the surface.

"A man shouldn't have to go without!"

His food suddenly forgotten, he watched Chioe's every movement through the open door as she led her horse out from the corral.

Jed Jones was angry with himself for having misjudged the stranger. He should not have invited him into his home, to sit at his table, to threaten his women. He cursed himself inwardly. He had dealt with backwoodsmen like Jango before – they only understood strength and had no code of civility. They were used to simply taking what they wanted and Jango's mind was now filled with desire for Chioe's body. Many years earlier, Jed had shared Indian women with his partner while trapping in the 'far country' – but that was different. The tribes had offered the women in exchange for fresh meat, so it was a fair trade; they would have been offended by any refusal.

Looking directly at Jango, he said: "You've got no chance there, son. She's Sasquatchoni. She'll cut your balls off!"

"I'm willing to take the chance," said Jango. His thumbs were hooked over the table edge and he was about to stand up.

"Maybe you are, mister, but I'm not!" said Jed.

Before Jango could get any further he felt a painful jab in his crotch and he jerked backwards involuntarily.

Looking down he saw the barrel of Jed's Remington pointing at his groin.

"This says you don't, mister. I think you'd better leave!"

Jango stared back at Jed coldly as the color drained from his face. His unblinking eyes projected intense hatred at the older man as he struggled to control his temper. His jaw clamped tight and his fingers balled into iron-hard fists.

"You old fool!" he exploded, pushing himself away from the table. "She's only an Indian and you're just a squawman, you old shit! They don't count for nothing!"

Jed knew he had to make a decisive move. In one swift action he swang the butt of his rifle around and cracked it with sickening force against the side of Jango's head. Lady was standing with her back to the fire range. She held her face in shock at the unexpected violence she had just witnessed from her husband. She watched, numb, as Jed's rifle fell once more.

After an hour or so, Jed threw a bucket of cold water over the unconscious man and stood back a couple of paces. The soaking washed some of the caked blood from Jango's face and managed to revive him a little.

"Get up and move out!" he commanded.

When Jango responded only slowly, Jed kicked him viciously in the ribs and grabbed his shirt, hauling him erect. Jango groaned, his legs flailing beneath him as the old trapper dragged him to the open door and heaved him outside. Breathing hard with the effort, he threw Jango's empty rifle on top of his outstretched body.

"Now git, you little bastard! If I catch you 'round my place again, I'll have the hide off your back!"

The urgent need to leave made Jango almost oblivious to the pain until he touched the raw swelling on the side of his busted head. As he withdrew his hand from the wound he winced at the sight of the dark red blood on his fingers.

Groggily, he climbed to his feet and staggered away.

"How long before we reach the trading post, major?" enquired the first sergeant, wearily.

Major Tim O'Hara spat the twig he had been chewing into the dust, glad that the routine patrol was nearing its end. He pulled his fob watch from his pocket.

"Another two hours, or thereabouts."

The first sergeant continued: "I think the horses have cooled down enough now, sir."

O'Hara looked at him. "Yep, I agree with you, Joe."

He straightened his hat, pulled the cinch tighter and swung himself up onto his horse's saddle. The sergeant yelled his commands to the rest of the troop and they set off.

"Well, major! Long time no see!" said Jed.

"Hold on there, Mister Jones. Why are you being so formal?" O'Hara snapped his fingers. "Oh, I've got it! You've forgotten my name. It's Tim, remember?"

"Timmo! Sure, I remember you - you Irish hooligan!" replied Jed.

Both men laughed uproariously at their little game, before shaking hands warmly and clumping each other around the shoulders.

"I had you spotted way back there, Tim – you was raising more dust than a herd of buffalo."

"Knew I wouldn't catch you by surprise, Jed."

"You're damn right, Tim. It took me a lot of learning and mistakes - all the hell and back pain of it - before I got it figured. Ignore the warning signs out here, and you're a dead man."

"Had any trouble?" asked O'Hara.

"Naw, nothing I can't handle."

O'Hara turned to the soldier behind him. "Sergeant – dismount the troops!"

"Say, Tim – would you do me a good turn?"

"Surely, name it."

"Well, I've got a young Sasquatchoni girl called Chioe staying here. She came in to do some trading and… well… I've known her all her born days. Truth is, I kinda think of her as m'own."

"Would that be Chief Tonala's daughter?" O'Hara interjected. "It so happens, we're stopping at her father's camp on the way back."

"Couldn't be better!" exclaimed Jed. "'Course, she won't like it - riding with you, I mean. But the thing is - there's a horny trapper round these parts who's got himself a yearning for an Indian woman."

O'Hara nodded his head in comprehension.

Jed's demeanour changed and he slapped his hand against his head with a look of disgust on his face. "Now, what sort of a host am I? C'mon into the store, Tim. Got m'self some good malt whiskey! Will you join me?"

"Thought you'd never ask," said O'Hara.

"C'mon sergeant, I got a jar for the boys that'll lay the dust, and then some," said Jed, leading the way.

* * * *

The smaller of the two dark-haired creatures turned

and spoke to the huge male standing nearby.

"RoShann, I feel the cold!" she said.

He knew she was not referring to the coolness of the forest, for his own body was also beginning to feel chilled. Glancing up through the tall pine trees he could see the golden morning sun. It was climbing higher. As they walked between the aged trees, shafts of warm sunlight filtered through the foliage, gilding their reddish brown fur. Despite their exertions the temperature of their bodies continued to fall.

"Come, Concilla - we will hide near the camp of the white man."

Soon, the two creatures had discovered Jango's horses tethered near the bank of a river. His pack and cooking utensils were scattered near an unlit pile of firewood.

Sometime later, an exceptionally tall, naked Indian emerged from the thick brush. A quick look around assured him that Jango's two horses were still grazing. With an urgent gesture, he beckoned to the young woman behind him. "We must hurry!"

They both plunged into the river and washed themselves vigorously. The water was pure and fast flowing and they took the opportunity to drink deeply, cupping it in their hands.

When they were done, the man heaved himself onto the riverbank and turned to help the woman climb out. As she emerged from the water she placed her arms around her companion, hugging him tightly against her body.

They kissed passionately. Her sensitive brown eyes stared at the man. "I love you!" she murmured.

Holding the woman close to him, he answered softly, "I know."

Pleased by the simple statement the woman gave a broad smile. The moment passed, and it was time to pull on the few garments they had carried with them.

* * * *

Jango was suffering from concussion. He had no idea how long he had been unconscious. Rolling over onto his back he stared at the sun. It was directly overhead. "Noon!" he croaked. "Oh, God!"

He lay motionless, one arm thrown carelessly across his face. Fighting back waves of nausea that threatened to overwhelm him, he levered himself upright using his empty rifle as a prop and managed to stagger to his feet. Leaning forward, he forced himself to walk.

In his delirious state of mind, the forest the creatures

had chased him from now seemed to take on a mantle of menace. A cooling breeze rustled the branches of the swaying trees. He watched a startled woodchuck race away. He desperately wanted to see something familiar. Anxiously, he approached his camp.

"The horses are gone! The goddam horses are gone!"

Slowly, the full implications of what that meant came home to him. *'A man is nothing without a horse.'* His face creased with fury, a savage cry of pent-up frustration wrenched itself from his lungs. "No-o-o-oh!"

Falling to his knees he slammed his fist into the earth, repeatedly. When his energy was spent, he collapsed onto his side and rolled down the bank into the river. He submerged briefly before wrenching his head up out of the shallow water, gasping for breath. Bereft, he sat for some time in the cool stream before clambering out, soaked to the skin.

Picking up some small rocks, he hurled them one by one into the dark green pine trees. "Yeh bastards! Yeh goddam stinking bastards!"

Exhausted at last, Jango sat reflecting quietly on his loss. Like a seedling taking root in fertile ground a thought grew rapidly in size until it became his only hope: *'There's just one person around here who has horses - I could get replacements from him.'*

Frantically, he reached into his pack and searched for his last two bullets. He remembered carefully wrapping them in a piece of cloth – where were they?

He released a sigh of satisfaction as he found them. With a renewed sense of purpose, he began cleaning his rifle.

O'Hara had just finished shaving when the aroma of spicy coffee wafted along on the soft morning breeze. Running his tongue around his lips, he swallowed hard.

The barn door creaked open and old Jed stepped through. "Kinda guessed you'd like some of this!" He proffered a steaming tin mug to O'Hara. The major began sipping the hot black liquid gratefully.

"Thanks, Jed. I sure as hell needed that," he said. Throwing the last of the coffee grouts onto the floor, and without waiting for a reply, he continued: "Is the girl ready? We'll be leaving in thirty minutes."

Having said *'Adios'* to Jed, O'Hara led the column out with Chioe by his side, heading for Chief Tonala's camp.

Jed had a late breakfast. He finished the last of his

coffee, wiped his mouth across the back of his hand and smiled at his wife.

"I enjoyed that, Lady." She nodded her head, pleased that she could satisfy her man in such an easy way. "O'Hara and his men were good company, for a while. Sometimes I wish it was like it used to be. Just you an' me!" He paused and breathed out a deep sigh. "Those days are gone and we'll never see their like again!" Jed's voice and face mirrored his sadness. "We travelled all over this durn country, didn't we – eh? Shootin' an' skinnin', out there alone. How long we two bin together, Lady?"

She touched his white hair and gently ran her fingers through the thinning strands. "Many winters, Jed - when this was blood red. If the buffalo should come back, we two – why, we would be too old to trail." Lady reached out and caressed Jed's big hands - hands that were rough, but which could, at times, be so gentle. She looked at the brown age spots mottling their backs.

"Yep. I didn't need nobody else, after I took you as a wife. Best durn bargain a man ever made."

"People need the company of others to survive, that is Indian wisdom!" said Lady.

A sudden ruckus from outside startled the old trader. He knocked the chair sideways as he grabbed at his rifle.

Through the open doorway he scanned the area of land visible from the trading post, as far as the near horizon. He could see nothing. "Well, I'll be…!" he exclaimed, noticing the dislodged corral posts. "It's okay Lady, it's just that frisky stallion; he's still mountin' the mare." He watched the stallion sink its teeth into the mare's neck for better leverage. "Durn that horse, I was hoping somebody would make a trade for him. Reckon I'd better put up those poles agin, Lady, afore they skedaddle."

Laying down his rifle, Jed strode through the doorway.

'A man that wants to survive out here shouldn't ignore any signs.' In the second that it took to exit the doorway, Jed realised he had broken one of his own cardinal rules. On the left of the trading post was a small wooded area covered with thick brush that was a roost for a turkey hen and her chicks - but there was no sign of them. Smaller birds were flying high, sounding their alarm.

An indefinable feeling came over old Jed - a sixth sense that told him something fateful was about to occur. In a flash, he knew with certainty that his time was about to be called. A lifetime of hunting and trapping, taking chances, had enlivened his senses to a fine pitch. He had often noted how creatures of the wild seemed to know when their death was imminent.

Four strides from the safety of the trading post and his rifle, Jed paused, stretched out his arms and faked a yawn. He had to look unconcerned; he knew that. On the fifth step, he turned on his heel and threw himself desperately towards the door. *'I'm gonna make it!'*

Jed heard the explosion, but experienced no pain. The bullet caught him in the neck and he collapsed, face forwards, like an old buffalo.

He could hear Lady screaming, could feel hands turning him over and holding his head. *'Goddam eyes are wide open, yet I can't see? Strange that!'*

"Jed! Jed!" Lady was crying.

'Stop your bellowing woman, dying ain't so bad!'

Alarmed by her husband's silence and his loss of blood, Lady understood that her worst fears had come true and began at once to chant the death song of a passing warrior.

Jed was aware of her tears striking his face.

The next shot sent the birds soaring into the air again and Jed was conscious of Lady falling across him.

Jango held the empty rifle steady. Though he knew instinctively that Jed and Lady were both dead, still he moved warily, alert to possibilities. It was some three hours since the troopers had left, taking the Sasquatchoni girl with them. He figured they would be too far down the trail to have heard the shots. He took a quick look around the post and then he approached the bodies.

"I'm sorry Lady, but I had to do it because yuh wouldn't have let up!" he rasped belligerently.

"'Twas your old man's fault, anyways, him a squawman as well, old bastard."

Jango moaned as he touched his bruised face and the ear that would be permanently swollen. He walked over to the corral and gathered the two mares. The stallion danced away, screaming in defiance. "I don't want you anyway, old son, you're more damned trouble than you're worth!" Throwing a saddle onto one horse and a pack harness onto the other, Jango tied them to the hitching post.

There was one other thing he needed before he left. Searching frantically, he soon located Jed's moneybag. "Whoo-eee! Paydirt at last!" Working quickly, Jango loaded up the money, some ammunition and anything else he thought might prove useful on the trail. Grabbing a piece of sourdough bread he chewed on it hungrily and washed it down with leftover coffee.

As he looked around the rough-timbered walls of Jed's cabin his gaze came to a halt above the fire range. His eyes narrowed: "A Shawnee tomahawk!" A lopsided grin split his face. "Yeah, why not?" Placing the tomahawk alongside the bodies he tested the sharpness of his skinning knife with the edge of his thumb. "I bet you took plenty of hair in your day, Jed, uh? Well, now it's your turn old man."

Jango threw the two scalps into the trading post. "How d'you like that, Jed? You're riding to the happy hunting ground with no hair, yuh bald headed old bastard!"

Chuckling at his morbid sense of humour he dipped his hands into the water butt and went back inside the trading post. With a cigar clamped firmly between his teeth, he looked around until he found a can of coal oil and then proceeded to scatter it about willy-nilly. Crossing to the fire range he pulled out a smouldering ember. Lighting his cigar, he walked outside and tossed the burning wood over his shoulder.

Jango casually mounted his horse, kicked hard, and rode off with the packhorse trailing behind him.

3. IN SEARCH OF EAGLE FEATHERS

RoShann and Concilla stopped for a while to rest the horses. They had ascended a ridge and were now high enough to look down upon a sweeping expanse of prairie land.

RoShann turned to his wife and said proudly: "We are now in the Sasquatchoni hunting grounds. All this land belongs to my tribe!" He pointed out the spacious lodges and the farmland his people tilled. Lines of crops were just visible outside the Indian camp. With an outstretched arm he indicated the distant location of the small settlement founded by the white men, now blossoming into a town.

Concilla's apprehension at the thought of meeting the elders of her husband's tribe showed on her face. She bit her lower lip and blurted out her fears hurriedly. "RoShann, will your family accept me? I am not of your tribe - will they like me?"

He gave her a reassuring grin. "Concilla, when you became my wife, you became a Sasquatchoni woman. My mother will welcome you as a daughter and love you for making her work lighter. You will impress them, have no fear."

Then he leaned close to her, whispering conspiratorially: "But I think it would be best not to talk about the valley, or the herb. If we do, people will think we are suffering from sun sickness, or that we are trying to make fools of them. That can wait for another day."

Smiling broadly he lifted her onto her horse. "Come, let us continue. My father, Tonala, will want to see his son's wife!"

Two hours later, they crossed the perimeter of the tribal camp. An old woman observed their entrance and exclaimed excitedly: "RoShann! He has returned!"

"Welcome back, RoShann!" called another.

They were now approaching the main avenue of the village. Young boys raced with each other to be first with the news: "RoShann is back! RoShann has returned with a wife!"

As word spread from lodge to lodge, people turned out to see RoShann and the newcomer to the tribe. They shouted their greetings to the couple as they rode past.

Soon, the pair had reached the clearing in front of the Sasquatchoni chieftain's lodge, now full of tribesmen.

Dismounting his horse, RoShann grabbed his mother and swung her high into the air. She held tight and showered his face with kisses. "RoShann, we thought you were dead!" she said, with tears streaming down her face. "You have been gone one whole winter!"

Tonala clasped them both in his arms; his affection for his family was obvious to everyone. "You were always in our thoughts, my son. Your absence was felt by every member of the tribe." He indicated the assembled throng with a wave of his hand and then paused. "We prayed for the return of our son and are glad that the Spirits have answered us - but you have returned with a woman?"

Concilla pushed her way through the crowd of curious people, until she stood beside RoShann. He immediately placed a protective arm around her shoulder.

"She is called Concilla, and her tribe are the Osage!"

The joyful meeting was cause for celebration amongst the Sasquatchoni people. They relished the prospect of the feasting that would follow upon the return of a favourite son and the many stories he would have to tell. But a warrior pointing to the far end of the village interrupted the greeting ceremony. He sounded the alarm: "Soldiers!"

With all the excitement and attention focused upon

RoShann, the sentinels had neglected the eastern approach. The shouted exclamation was picked up and passed amongst the people like a prairie breeze.

"It's Chioe and the major!"

A pathway opened for the riders as they swept into the settlement, only to be instantly filled again by the milling crowd.

"Welcome to our camp, major!"

O'Hara wiped away the trail dust with his kerchief. "Thank you, Tonala. My apologies for intruding on your celebrations, but I have some urgent business to conclude: the safe delivery of your beautiful daughter."

He gestured toward Chioe, who smiled at the compliment. As she dismounted from her horse, she caught sight of her brother and called out in surprise. "RoShann!" She ran forwards and threw herself into his arms.

Having paid his respects to Tonala, O'Hara eased himself from his saddle and strode over to RoShann. He gripped the young warrior's hand. "It's a pleasure to see you again, RoShann."

After a brief discussion they came to an agreement: Tonala would come to the fort on the day of the full moon.

"You will stay with us, major?" requested Tonala.

"We celebrate my son's return."

"There's nothing I'd like better, Tonala – but, unfortunately, I have to return with my men to Fort Kearny." He nodded in the direction of the waiting troopers. "Colonel Austin is a stickler for the rules."

Mounting his horse, O'Hara saluted. Tonala watched as his people parted their ranks; once clear of the crowd the jogging horse broke into a canter.

Throughout the day the young couple received friends and relations, all of whom brought gifts, each trying to surpass the other in their generosity. Whilst visiting RoShann, the men took the opportunity to admire the youthful body of his woman. They were sure she would bear him many strong sons.

The light began to fade. At last, the festivities could begin. The darkness receded before the glow of the numerous cooking fires; sparks showered into the black night, borne away on a gentle breeze. Soon, a rich mixture of smells saturated the air; cooking pots boiled over and melting fat dripped onto sizzling fires. The sour, sweated odours of the assembled men mingled with those of the animal fats and permeated the air. Dogs barked and fought with each other for discarded food scraps; people laughed and talked as they watched their children play chasing games.

In a respectful tone, RoShann began to speak: "Father, do you remember the day I came of age, when you gave me your black stallion as a token of my manhood?"

Tonala was carefully packing tobacco into his favorite smoking pipe. It was a well-crafted object, beautifully inlaid with strips of silver and gold. "You still have the stallion, my son. It belongs to you," he answered.

Pausing while his father got the smoking pipe well and truly alight, RoShann continued: "Long ago, you taught me that the honour of a gift should be repaid. I was determined that Tonala should have a gift that would enhance his position as chief of the Sasquatchoni people. So… I have brought you a cloak made from eagle feathers!"

The assembled warriors roared their approval. One of the oldest filled his lungs with smoke before passing the pipe on. "The son of Tonala speaks wise words," he croaked. "But where did you find the feathers, RoShann? It is well-known that eagles nest only amongst the highest rocks of the highest mountains. No man has ever climbed so high!"

RoShann smiled at the enquiry. "I will tell you of my adventure. The parts of it I can tell you now are strange enough; other parts, perhaps, should never be told."

The men fell silent and listened to RoShann as he started to relate his tale.

"One morning I awoke from a deep sleep and lay in the darkness, unable to clear my head of mystical visions. I had asked the spirits to show me how I should honour my father. Whilst asleep, I had dreamed of finding an eagle's nest. I took it as a sign – and, therefore, decided to find an eagle's nest that very day. I would fashion the finest cloak ever made from an eagle's feathers.

I rose from my bed and raised my arms to the Great Spirit. I sang a sacred song to our brother the sun, pleading with him to break free from Mother Earth, so that he might show me the way with his light and warmth. This, he did... I set forth, sure that Manitou would guide me on my quest..."

* * * *

The eagle's talons dug firmly into the soft flesh of the squealing jackrabbit and its huge wings began to beat slowly, groping for a corridor of warm air that would help lift its heavy body from the flat prairie lands. Wheeling around, it rode the air currents until it soared upwards again. Clutching its prey tightly, it gained height rapidly and headed for Snow Mountain.

Shading his eyes from the burning glare of the sun, RoShann watched the eagle's progress, mentally marking out the trail he would have to follow in pursuit. *"Shoshone country!"*

He knew his father would be proud to possess the plumage of such a skillful hunter, a sky spirit, full of courage. On any ordinary hunting trip he would have brought his rifle, but this was a special task: he had sworn to kill the eagle with his bare hands.

After only four days of tracking and searching he was pleased to have found his quarry so quickly. The eagle had headed for a particular part of the mountain and he would follow, whatever the difficulties. His aching legs reminded him of how much he missed his young stallion, but this was no terrain for an untrained horse; the trail was far too rocky. He decided to walk on towards Snow Mountain while the light of day held.

As twilight suffused the landscape he noticed a river nearby. The swift running water looked inviting. Glancing down at his body he saw rivulets of perspiration descending through a coating of fine red trail dust. He stood quietly in the warm air and listened, trying to identify every sound. His eyes peered ahead at the densely knotted brush, looking for any trace of danger. Reassured at last that no one could surprise him, he began to undress.

Standing on the edge of the river, RoShann revelled in his nakedness. Placing his feet carefully, he walked slowly into the water. The numbing coldness caught him by surprise, making him inhale great draughts of air. Gradually, his body acclimatized to the chill and he began to enjoy the water. Pushing his arms out and kicking his legs, he swam around at a leisurely pace. He was pleased with the day's progress and had a great sense of contentment. Turning over onto his back he relaxed as he gazed up at the hypnotic blood-red orb of the setting sun. He felt like a spirit floating through the heavens.

When the day's dust was washed from his body, he climbed out and settled down for the night.

In a trance-like state, he watched the sun slowly disappear behind the mountains. Then he closed his eyes and fell into a dreamless sleep.

He awoke with a jolt, instantly alert and aware that he was in unfamiliar territory. It was not wise to sleep through the dawn. The sun's luminous glow had not yet broken through a heavy layer of cloud and the air was still cool. The local population of birds amused him with their whistling and nattering as they waited patiently for the first rays of daylight. Their calling continued unabated as the sun rose.

Sitting down again, RoShann breakfasted on dried pemmican and fruits, washed down with gulps of cold water. He gathered together his weapons and filled his waterskin pouch. As he did so, he looked resolutely at the Snow Mountain range, five or six miles away. He was determined to reach it.

He looked around his camp once more; he would have preferred to rest longer, but there was a hard climb ahead. Shrugging his shoulders, he pushed his way through the scrub.

Breathing hard, he paused for a moment to wipe the sweat from his brow. RoShann had never climbed a mountain before and had little knowledge of the difficulties he might have to overcome. But he was young and eager to test himself: to climb the mountain alone would be a feat to be proud of, and there were no elders around to counsel him against the idea. As he continued to walk toward the mountain the ground began to rise above the surrounding plain. The sun seemed to climb with him.

Looking up at the rock face ahead it seemed an impossible task. He flexed his arms and fingers as he massaged the pain in his aching legs. As he viewed the sun's position he shook his head: "Half a day gone - it looked so easy!' He gulped down some water and dowsed his head to cool off, then waited a while as his breathing slowed and his mind began to clear. Refreshed again, he attacked the mountain with renewed vigour.

By late afternoon his limbs were weary and he had risen to a considerable height by ascending a steep crag. He knew he was close to the eagle's nest and his eyesight was good – but still he could not see it. He scrutinized the rocks, fissures and promontories, searching for any trace of the elusive nest.

Suddenly - "Ah, there it is!"

He pulled himself up on to a ledge; every muscle in his large body ached, but he found new zest for the task when he reminded himself of the tales he would be able to tell about this day. As he fought to regain his breath he stared at the large, sprawling nest. It was skillfully constructed from interleaved twigs and was surrounded by downy feathers and the whitened bones of former meals. Within it sat the sole occupant: a small, scrawny, eaglet.

"Ha! You are not worth this hard climb!" He slapped his thigh and laughed at the thought flashing through his mind: *"This bird wouldn't even make a good bowl of soup!"*

He stood for a moment, transfixed by the stunning panorama before him, a scene of breathtaking beauty. Although the scenery was wondrous he could not allow himself to fully relax. At any moment, the mother eagle might return, and he had to remain alert to the peril. He moved behind an outcrop of rock to spare his eyes from the more severe rays of the burning sun and managed to pick out the wooded area where he had spent the night. It was so far away - and it seemed very small.

As he surveyed the rolling plains beyond the rivers and lakes, RoShann envied the eagle for its power of flight, its keen eyesight and its effortless majesty. An unsettling thought occurred to him: the people of his tribe were reckoned by the other Indian nations to be giants. And it was true; the average Sasquatchoni male was many hands higher than other men, and only the most robust horses could carry their weight. RoShann himself was the tallest of the tall, and amongst the strongest. But as he stood on the ledge halfway up Snow Mountain, he felt very insignificant and diminished. At that precise moment he came to a decision: "I will not kill the eagle. Its spirit belongs to the mountain."

In his distracted state, the return of the parent bird caught him by surprise. Her hunting trip had proved fruitless and she had flown back to the nest to check on the eaglet. She was enraged to find that a man-animal had invaded her nest. She attacked him immediately.

Coming in fast she struck at RoShann, her talons

raking his shoulders, her heavy wings beating him frantically about the head in an attempt to topple him. He reacted automatically, punching his arms in the air and crouching low in an effort to shield his face. Instinctively, he threw himself backwards into a spiny bush that sprouted from a deep recess in the rock face. Despite his pledge, he reached for his hunting knife; he was sure the eagle would recover from its surprise plunge and soar upwards to gather height before attacking him again. He tensed, brandishing his knife, waiting for the next onslaught.

But instead, the great bird simply landed and settled next to the young eaglet, seemingly content that the man had retreated and the chick was alive.

RoShann sheathed his knife: he was tired and his desire to kill the bird had waned. He would gain no honours here...

He was at a loss for what to do next, when a cool draught of air moved across his skin and made him turn to investigate the cleft in the rock face. There seemed to be a cavity behind the narrow opening, perhaps a cave. He did not feel he had the strength to descend from the mountain before nightfall and if he could find shelter on the ledge then it would be better to stay there until morning.

His mind was set upon the new task, and he worked

energetically to pull away the loose rocks around the hole, enlarging the gap until it was big enough for him to force his body through. Before entering the darkness beyond, he collected all the dead wood he could find and pushed it into the opening. Now, all he needed was a torch. He untied his small pack and found some kindling. Working his fire-stick vigorously, he watched as the smoke burst into flame, whereupon, he quickly fashioned a burning brand. With some effort, he succeeded in squeezing through the gap and found himself stumbling across a dirt floor.

With his torch well and truly alight he probed the dark recesses of the cave, his shadow looming grotesquely on the wall. He was curious as to where the draught of air was coming from. The cave receded into a narrow passage at the rear, and it was so dark the light from the fluttering torch did little to illuminate it. With hunger pangs coming upon him he resolved to leave further exploration until the morning. Satisfied that the cave was home to no particular animal, he made a fire and ate the last of his food. He wanted the fire to burn all night, so he ensured that it was well built-up and then made himself comfortable under a thin blanket. Soon, he had drifted off into a deep, exhausted, sleep.

Throwing back his covering, RoShann yawned and stretched his arms upwards. He grimaced with sudden pain as the dry lacerations on his chest and shoulders broke open. The eagle had punished him severely for his impudence. Ignoring the claw marks, he began making torches, utilizing strips of cloth torn from his blanket. He knew that he could not go far into the cave; he would need most of his strength to descend from the mountain and he would have to make good use of the daylight. He decided that he could always return another day if the cave was worth examining further. For now, it would suffice just to scout around. Treading carefully, he made his way along the passage, his curiosity intensifying. Would it lead up or down?

As he proceeded deeper into the mountainside, the rocks above lowered and a strong rush of cold air blew out the torch. He groped blindly until his left hand touched the rocks at his side and he was able to orientate himself. He was not unduly alarmed as he felt he could reverse his tracks and find the entrance again fairly easily. With one foot probing the ground ahead he advanced cautiously into the blackness, straining his eyes for any small pinprick of daylight. There had to be another entrance ahead, somewhere; he could sense it.

So impenetrable was the darkness his imagination began to play tricks on him; images of people and animals appeared and disappeared before him. His reason told him they were unreal. Rubbing his eyes, he momentarily forgot his wariness and stepped forwards.

Suddenly he was falling, twisting and turning in space; he had tumbled into some kind of shaft. RoShann was certain that his death was imminent; a desolate thought flashed through his mind: *'Nobody will ever know what happened to me.'*

A surge of ice-cold water enveloped him and he held his breath involuntarily. Desperately, he struggled to right himself – but which way was up? Kicking out powerfully, he broke through the surface of the water, coughing and spitting as he sucked in great lungfuls of air. Rolling over onto his back he pushed out his arms – he touched a rock ceiling. He could see nothing; the darkness was total. Breathing more easily now, but completely helpless, he had no choice but to drift with the current.

The flow of water bore him along quite swiftly, occasionally bumping him against the rough sidewalls as it followed its tortuous course. Bruised and chilled to the bone, RoShann wondered if he would ever see daylight again. Disorientated, he tried to compose himself. *'Is this really happening? Is my imagination playing games with me?'* Again, his head bumped against the low, jagged roof and he cried out in pain; there was nothing he could do, but try to outlive the ordeal. He took a sharp gulp of air as the rocky ceiling met the water and he was forcibly submerged. With no choice but to drown or to find an air pocket, he swam beneath the surface, silently praying to the Great Spirit for deliverance, or a quick death.

'Yes, it gets lighter!' RoShann clung to the last vestiges of his consciousness. His face was beginning to contort through lack of oxygen and he slowly released blobs of precious air to ease the pressure within his bursting lungs. *'Light!'*

He urged his tired body on: *'Green weeds growing!'*

Struggling violently to contain his breath, the light faded and he lost consciousness.

Dimly, from a faraway place, RoShann became aware of people standing around him. They were straining to lift his heavy body clear of the water, and working vigorously to pump the liquid from his lungs. In his traumatized state, it seemed as though a whole tribe of people were jumping on his back and massaging his limbs.

IN SEARCH OF EAGLE FEATHERS

* * * *

Slowly, RoShann's sense of smell returned and his nostrils flared at the rancid atmosphere of the enclosed tepee in which he found himself. He sat up and stared into the startled brown eyes of a young woman as she leaned over him. She immediately shrank back in fright and rose to her feet. Moving away, she lifted the skins covering the tent entrance and hurriedly walked out.

It seemed to RoShann that a long time had passed since the young squaw had left him alone. When he next opened his eyes he was surprised to find a young boy staring at him warily from the entrance. The boy hesitated, and then beckoned him to follow as he walked outside.

Throwing off the buffalo robe, RoShann struggled to stand. He staggered and stumbled onto his knees as a groan escaped from his clenched jaws, but with an effort of will he managed to push himself up to his full height. The boy backed off and fled, his nerve deserting him.

Once outside, the fresh morning air revived RoShann and he breathed deeply. He could detect the pungent tang of wood smoke and he saw two women tending a fire with some children standing nearby. As he stood there the beauty of the surrounding landscape took his attention.

The tepee seemed to be located in a green mountain valley. From its location he could look down the length of the valley, but he could not make out the far end. The air was colder than he was used to and when the heavy swirling mist cleared he could see the valley was ridged on both sides by snow-capped mountains. He noticed the absence of animals in the small camp; he could see no horses, no dogs. Perhaps they were kept elsewhere? The valley was lush and fertile, quite unlike the plains he was used to.

He walked over to the women. As he approached, the older squaw rose and turned towards him. Silently, she pointed at a large, red tepee. The gesture needed no comment, so he bent low to enter the dwelling.

Inside, he found a warrior, sitting alone. The man acknowledged his presence with a sweep of his arm to indicate that RoShann should sit on the left, in the guest position. Indian etiquette would normally have demanded the expression of formal greetings, together with an exchange of gifts, but RoShann was not in a position to offer anything and his host obviously wished to set him at ease. The two women entered the tepee and placed a meal in front of the men: hot maize cakes, sliced meats and bowls of hot drinks flavoured with red currants.

The silence was briefly disturbed by the shrill yells of the children as they raced each other into the tepee, only to be quickly scolded and hushed by the older squaw. This done, the women and children took their places on the right of the tepee.

The warrior cleared his throat. He was older than RoShann, old enough to pray to the spirit of his father. "I am Red Horse of the Osage tribe," he said. "This is my squaw, Neli, the mother of my children, and that -" he nodded his head at the younger woman – "is her sister, Concilla. I bid you welcome to our home."

Red Horse twisted around and picked up a small child wrapped in swaddling. He undid the binding and the baby crawled out into its father's arms. He hugged the child close to him and chuckled. "A man cannot be serious when he holds such charms." He caressed the child and kissed its face before handing it back to his squaw. Red Horse then pointed at the four children. "They are my tribe. Small, but fearsome!" He laughed again.

RoShann took the opportunity to introduce himself. He struck his chest with a clenched fist and said simply, "I am RoShann of the Sasquatchoni." It was a flat statement, but his voice was full of pride. "I am grateful for the care you have given me, and the food that you offer. I shall make an offering to the Great Spirit in your name, that you may be blessed with many sons."

Red Horse tilted his head. "Sasquatchoni? I have

heard stories of your tribe. Brave warriors who are feared and respected by all!"

Red Horse picked up a piece of meat and offered it to RoShann, who accepted it gladly. It was the signal for them all to begin eating.

When the meal was over and everyone's hunger had been satisfied, RoShann told the small gathering about his quest to find the eagle, and his subsequent brush with death. They all listened attentively.

"... So that is how I came to be here. I climbed the mountain, fell down a shaft, and found myself in this green and fertile valley with my life indebted to an Osage warrior. I have been fortunate in meeting you, Red Horse - without your help I may have drowned. But there is something I do not understand. I have been to the Osage homelands and they are many days away from the mountains. This is a special place, but I have never heard it spoken of amongst my people. You must surely have a tale to tell."

Red Horse was unwilling to be drawn by the enquiry. "You speak the truth, my brother. This is indeed a special place - a sacred place. This valley has become our refuge from the white man, and its secret must remain ours alone."

The declaration seemed to be Red Horse's final word,

but he continued. "You are welcome to stay with us for as long as you wish. This land is rich and we want for nothing. Life is good here, as you see. The outside world does not disturb us. When you have recovered from your injuries you will want to return to your people. I understand that. But heed my words: there is only one way out of the valley – a high pass between two peaks. I warn you now: Do not try to leave, without taking me as your guide. There is always snow up there, deep snow. The mountain is so high it steals a man's breath away and every mouthful of air you breathe will paralyse your lungs. It is so intensely cold your limbs will freeze. Great strength is needed just to push oneself forward. There is great risk of death."

RoShann wondered why the Osage was being so dramatic and why he was so cautious. And what 'secret' was he referring to? He decided not to ask any further questions until he had explored the valley: he would find his own way out, in time. Nevertheless, he resolved to indulge the Osage warrior in this game of question and answer, for it was obvious that Red Horse was savouring the web of mystery he had spun around his own arrival in the valley. How had an Osage family established itself here? To live in isolation was alien to their way of life; they were tribal people like the Sasquatchoni, dependent on custom, lore and on each other. A small family was vulnerable to attacks from marauders; there were always bands of young warriors around, looking for blood and. conquest. Was that why Red Horse would not part with his knowledge of the valley? Perhaps he was waiting until he could be sure of RoShann's character?

Red Horse could sense the curiosity of the young Sasquatchoni and suggested that he rest for one more day. "Take these gifts," he said, offering RoShann a blanket, a knife and a tomahawk. Nodding directly at the women, he said: "They will make you a shirt and some leggings."

RoShann had already noticed the younger woman. Her hair was combed and clipped in a style that proclaimed she was unmarried. The women were eager to show their skill at making clothes and they set about their task with great proficiency as Red Horse watched. They made RoShann sit for them as they held soft cured deerskins against his frame. Complex shapes were measured against the broadness of his back and marked out on the skins. Standing upright at the women's request, wearing only a breechclout, RoShann was unaware of the admiring glances the women exchanged behind his back. His bulk and. height filled the dilapidated tepee as both women gazed at him in awe. Cupping her hand, Neli whispered to Concilla who gave her sister a reproachful nudge. Smiling, they continued their work.

Red Horse had many questions to ask RoShann about recent events outside the valley and the women listened with interest as the Sasquatchoni did his best to answer. He described what had taken place in negotiations between the Indian tribes and the army administration. As Red Horse listened he began to trust RoShann more and felt that he understood the younger man. As the two talked they developed a rapport based on the common code of the hunter and an acceptance of each other's opinion.

When their conversation came to an end, both warriors stepped outside the tepee - Red Horse to hunt, RoShann to make his weapons.

Left alone in the tepee, the women carefully inspected the available skins before selecting the ones they would use for RoShann's clothing. Seated comfortably, they began their work, skillfully cutting and tacking the pieces.

"Neli!"

"What is it Concilla?" replied the older sister, without looking up from her work.

"I would like to make these clothes for RoShann, myself."

"Huh! So, you do like him?" Neli clapped her hands with joy, and laughed at her sister's embarrassment.

"Yes, yes I do," replied Concilla quietly. "If I make the clothes, then they would be a gift from me! But... you will say nothing?"

"Your secret is safe, Concilla," said Neli. "He is a handsome young warrior, and if Red Horse is away too long, I will throw myself at him and hold him down with these!" Neli held her fulsome breasts in both hands.

From the tepee came the screech of happy laughter. After a period of silent concentration, Concilla requested more from her sister. "What do you know of RoShann's tribe?" she said.

Neli shrugged her shoulders. "Only what one hears around the camp fires when old women gossip." Neli picked a wild plum from the bowl in front of her, and chewed on it contentedly. "As you have seen, the Sasquatchoni are the tallest warriors of any tribe - even the women are big, so they say." Although seated, Neli stretched a short arm above her head. "They have many possessions and good hunting grounds. I have heard they are fierce in war and never forget or forgive a wrong, and..."

Neli hesitated, searching desperately for the right words.

Concilla stopped her stitching and looked directly into her sister's eyes. "And what?" she prompted.

Neli spat out the plum stone and the words tumbled quickly from her lips: "A Sasquatchoni warrior never takes a wife from outside his own tribe!"

4. THE SECRET VALLEY

RoShann was now indebted to Red Horse for the gifts he had received, and was determined to repay him in some way, when he was able to do so. Standing outside the tepee he noticed that it had been repaired in many places - and that there was still no sign of horses or dogs. He could not conceive of an Indian family being without any form of transport; both creatures were commonly used for dragging loads, but Red Horse seemed to have no pack animals at all.

He asked himself the same question repeatedly: *'How did the Osage family enter this valley?'*

He recalled Red Horse's words: *'The only way out is through the snow.'* He shook his head disbelievingly, and vowed that he would not accept Red Horse's assertion until he had explored every possible pathway out of the valley.

He walked over to the river that had nearly cost him

his life and paused on the bank, staring at the water. It surged out strongly from beneath the rocky cliffs in a powerful torrent. He knew how fierce the underwater current was and he shuddered at the memory. It took no more than a few moments to assess the possibility of returning to the outside world that way: *'Impossible!'*

RoShann studied the mass of ancient rock towering above him; it was a beguiling picture of twisted and eroded shapes disgorged from the bowels of the fiery earth. Surrounding it was an untouched wilderness. His eyes drank in the colorful scene. At the lower levels of the valley he could see reddish-brown soil that ran into broad granite formations, some of which had a yellow cast. Green willows and cottonwoods clustered in swathes beneath towering cathedrals of rock, fringing their necks before merging into the borderline of snow. RoShann enjoyed the isolation of the valley and he felt in tune with the spirit of the wilderness.

He turned and followed the course of the river and was continually surprised by the different species of wildlife he encountered. He knew that in this land, a good hunter would never go hungry.

As he investigated the area he came across trees heavy with mature apples, and many varieties of bush laden with fruit. After some time walking he could see a large, still lake in the distance. The broadening river seemed to flow into it. He reasoned that the lake was not big enough to contain the waters of the river, so there had to be an overflow or outlet of some kind. Where did the water go?

Tracking along the riverbank, he stopped at a point thick with reeds and cupped his hands to taste the flavour of the water. As he paused, he noticed a muskrat toiling nearby to build its lodge. He could not resist having a closer look – but, on his approach, the animal dived swiftly back into the water. Alarmed at RoShann's intrusion, a flock of waterfowl ran on the river surface and flapped their wings until they caught the wind and took off, sounding their annoyance.

He had walked for longer than he had originally intended and he was suddenly stricken by pangs of hunger. He searched around and found what he was looking for; some crinkled leaves betrayed the presence of edible roots beneath the ground. He pulled them up and examined them. He thought he recognized them - turnip roots perhaps? Whatever they were, they had an acceptable flavour, and he consumed them greedily.

Having sated his hunger he looked around once more. The fast-flowing water had pounded the steep-sided valley for centuries and he observed that in several places it had washed recesses under the surrounding rock face. To satisfy his curiosity he dived in to explore them in more detail, even if only to confirm that there really was no way out. Treading water to keep himself afloat, he again pondered the question that kept returning to his mind: *'How did Red Horse and his family arrive here?'*

Wading ashore, he shivered in the cool evening air. His eyes lingered on the distant rim of the mountains, by now defined in sharp relief against the red-hued background of sunset. He would not resolve the mystery on this day...

On his way back to the tepee, RoShann cut a length of orange wood to make into a bow. He then selected some cherry saplings from which to fashion arrows. He would use the women's cooking fires to dry out the saplings when he returned to the camp - they had already promised to supply him with deer gut, flight feathers and glue. Red Horse had generously offered him some precious iron-tipped arrowheads, which would complete the task. Once the weapons were made, he would feel properly equipped and more like a warrior.

The family greeted him as his tall frame appeared at the entrance of their tepee. He was happy to take his place in the guest position once more, as the women set out an impressive array of food.

After the evening meal, Red Horse gazed into the fire, lost in thought. For two winters his family had lived in the valley, and despite some initial difficulties they had come to enjoy the conditions there. When all else was taken into consideration, he felt reasonably contented... but his mind was still unsettled. Although he did not like to dwell on such thoughts, at times he was afraid. He missed living within the traditions of the Osage tribe, where there was lore to provide assurance and advice. True, he had learned a few useful things from the old shaman before he died...

Ah, the shaman... The wise man named Tolmec. It was he who had led Red Horse to the valley. Elders such as Tolmec understood the spirits, knew how to use charms and healing potions. They could alleviate a man's fears with a few words. If only Tolmec was still alive. For Red Horse there was now no counsel but the recollection of his own experiences. The shaman had passed on his knowledge about the valley - and the secret of the bitter-tasting herbs that could entirely transform a man's body. Why the herbs brought about such a change was beyond Red Horse's comprehension. Perhaps he would learn more when he next had occasion to eat some? Once the drug had entered a warrior's bloodstream the strong medicine heightened his perception of all things.

Red Horse remembered with sadness the day the Osage tribal elders had decreed that the entire nation should confine itself to the reservation. His own view had been that such a move would destroy the tribe, as the white men would disarm the braves and rob them. He could not forget the harsh winter his family had endured in the camp before they finally abandoned it. He recalled that the whole tribe had been near starvation when the chief ordered the survivors to kill their horses to provide food. Many people had died; Neli lost two of her youngest children. Red Horse had watched them slowly die from hunger and disease, and he had even considered killing the remainder of his family if there was no other way to end their terrible suffering and humiliation. The chiefs of the white man had promised a constant supply of cattle in return for the Osage conceding more of their hunting grounds. He would never forget the feeling of betrayal the warriors had shared, when a small herd of starving cattle was driven to the reservation; it was clear to all of them that the animals were sick rejects that the white man no longer wanted. Instinctively, he and the other Osage warriors knew that this marked the end of their proud story: there would be no more tribal conflicts, no more striving to extend their power over other tribes; for they were prisoners now.

It was known by all of the tribes that the buffalo had gone, never to return. The plains people were no longer free to roam where their spirit took them. A warrior could still ride the prairie trails, but eventually he would cross a white man's ranch or some area of farmland; land that had once been freely traversed by members of Red Horse's nation.

In desperation, he and his family had packed their travois and left the encampment just a few days before the soldiers came. He remembered well the anguish he had suffered when he set the last of his horses free. Now, he would make many sacrifices to be able to ride a young horse again. There were lots of things he missed. Despite the relative safety and comfort of the valley, there were times when he ached for the company of his own people.

Since the death of Tolmec he had ventured outside the valley on only two or three occasions. His mind went back to the moment when he had discovered the shaman's seemingly lifeless body lying on a rugged escarpment near the mountains...

He had left Neli and the children to hunt for food, whilst they camped in the wild. They had fled from the reservation several days before and he had to forage continually to fend off his family's hunger. He had not expected to encounter any other Indian tribesmen in such a remote place and was startled when he first discovered what appeared to be the body of a tribal elder lying abandoned in a patch of long grass. At first, he thought the old man was dead, but a small movement of the reclining figure's hand signalled otherwise. He was wearing intricately twined necklaces and wrist bindings that signalled he was of high status. The decorated bone and bead adornments marked him out as a shaman – one who conversed with spirits. His face was frozen, his eyes closed.

Red Horse wondered if the man had lain there deliberately to welcome death. But on closer inspection that seemed not to be the case; for he noted with concern that the man had a bullet wound in his side. He had lost a lot of blood and it seemed likely that he would soon die, no matter what his story was. Nevertheless, Red Horse resolved to dignify his passing, so he carried the shaman to a sheltered spot between two large rocks and made a fire to keep him warm. He cleaned the old man's wound and kept him close to the fire until he regained consciousness. The shaman drank some water but did not speak and would not accept food. He was very weak. The night came quickly and Red Horse made the old man as comfortable as he could before settling down on the opposite side of the fire.

In the morning he awoke to find the shaman sitting

upright. The sleep seemed to have strengthened him a little and his voice was clear. Though old and injured, when he spoke he still conveyed authority and wisdom. He lifted his head and looked at Red Horse with a fixed gaze. In a firm tone he said he wanted to climb the nearby mountain.

"But you are dying!" objected Red Horse.

"Yes, I am. But according to Indian lore, a warrior is allowed to choose his last resting place, is he not?" Red Horse conceded the point with a slight nod of his head.

The dying man beckoned him to draw nearer and Red Horse complied, kneeling down before the shaman until their eyes locked together. The old man's face wore an absent expression as though part of his mind was adrift in a realm of painted dreams.

"You will help me to reach my chosen place. I, Tolmec the Shaman, have spoken."

Tolmec started searching through his pouch until he found what he was looking for. His fingers alighted upon their target and he sighed with satisfaction. He slowly withdrew his hand clutching some dried roots. The old medicine man began to chew on them slowly and offered a quantity to Red Horse. "Eat!" he urged.

Red Horse was accustomed to eating herbs of many kinds and in the wilderness that surrounded them there was little else to sustain a man, so he accepted the offering with gratitude. After just a few bites it was apparent that the herbs were bitter and unpleasant to taste, but the shaman commanded respect and Red Horse decided he would eat them without complaint. He wanted to spit out the roots, but his pride would not allow him to do so.

He began to feel warm and light-headed and then realized that he had begun to sweat profusely, though the sun was not high. Then his body began to tremble and he was wracked with a pain that caused him to convulse and writhe on the ground. His head was swimming; his eyes recorded nothing but illusions. Had the shaman poisoned him? He staggered to his feet and tried to walk. His body seemed to be suffocating for want of air. Frantically, he tore at his clothing and leggings, frightened at the change in his body. He looked at his legs and saw that they had begun to swell; then his arms were similarly affected. His limbs took on a bloated appearance and his skin screamed in burning agony at being stretched beyond its natural extent. Moving around in circles, he lost his balance and collapsed.

For a while he lay where he had fallen. Then he rolled over onto his hands and. knees, panting for breath like a dog. He heard Tolmec speaking to him calmly, reassuring him that all was well and that the pain would subside in a few moments. The shaman explained that the root was powerful medicine and that the swelling in Red Horse's limbs would give him extra strength and resistance to cold.

After the initial shock had worn off Red Horse regained his composure and acknowledged the encouraging words from Tolmec. He had been selected by the shaman to assist him in his quest to scale the mountain and he was determined to honour the appointment. He looked at the shaman and saw that Tolmec's body had also swollen to the point where he was barely recognizable as a man. But his voice was unchanged: "Come, let us go! The herbs will give us the strength to climb and my wound will be less troublesome while my body is like this. As we walk our bodies will grow hair. Do not be frightened, Red Horse. The effect is not permanent and it will decline in a few hours. The hair will fall out and you will once again become the son your mother knew – this, I promise. Now heed my words: we must reach my chosen resting place before the herbs lose their effect."

Tolmec moved more freely as they began to ascend the mountain slopes and he seemed less affected by the wound in his side, though it was still visible. Both men had removed most of their clothing and had packed their few possessions in pouches, which they slung loosely over their shoulders. The climb became more difficult as the rock faces steepened, but Red Horse marvelled at the way his body now responded. He felt much stronger than before and although his feet were bare, he felt no pain or cold from being in contact with the rock. Nor did the chill wind affect his back. He watched in fascination as the hair on his arms and body grew thicker as the day wore on, insulating him from the sun and the breeze. The two men made good progress and before the sun had climbed overhead they were approaching the snow line. As they did so, Tolmec began to struggle and fall behind. Red Horse went back to him. The wound in the shaman's side had opened again and his thick body hair was saturated with blood.

Red Horse gave him time to recover his breath, then said: "There is no dishonour in climbing upon the back of a strong horse, if one is available."

Tolmec looked at him though pained eyes. "If there is a willing horse, one would be a fool not to take advantage of it."

Higher and higher they climbed. With his newly acquired strength, the Osage warrior could barely feel the weight of the old man on his back. The shaman made no noise; he was asleep or unconscious. Red Horse could feel the warmth of his body on his back - which told him, at least, that his burden was alive. Suddenly, the old man woke, perhaps in response to some primitive instinct of homecoming that told him his birthplace was near. Stretching out a hand Tolmec pointed across the huge expanse of white snow ahead of them. "There is a cavern!" he gasped.

Red Horse experienced no particular awareness of passing from one side of the mountain to the other. They made their way through a steep-sided cleft, blanketed with snow. Enormous towering peaks disappeared into swirling mists that closed in and enveloped them, leaving droplets of moisture clinging to the thick growth of hair covering their bodies. The ground began to descend as Red Horse trudged forward through the mist, snow impeding his march.

All at once, as they emerged from the thick clouds, the scene before them changed; it was almost, thought Red Horse, as though he had just pulled aside the covering of his tepee. Spread before them was a wide, verdant valley. He stopped to absorb the sight, amazed to find such a lush, green refuge so high up in the mountain.

Some falling stones shook him from his reverie; on an outcrop of rock a small herd of bighorn sheep had stopped their browsing to stare at the newcomers. Once they had ascertained there was no need for alarm, they continued to feed.

"So this is the valley you spoke of, Tolmec?"

There was no reply.

"Tolmec!" Red Horse realized that the arms around his neck had gone limp and he wondered aloud: "Have I been carrying a dead man?" He glanced ahead and saw what he assumed was the cavern the old man had mentioned. Quickly, he made his way to the entrance.

The medicine man had warned him earlier of what could happen during the ascent: *'If my wound opens and the blood flows freely, my body will change rapidly. I will become a frail old man once again. When you begin to feel the cold, it is a sign that the effect of the herbs has been spent and you, too, will revert to your usual appearance. You will be, once again, a simple Osage warrior – one your mother would recognize.'*

He laid the shaman down gently inside the cavern entrance, and searched around for something to burn. He found an abundance of dry wood in an alcove and energetically worked his fire-stick in a bundle of wood shavings. Blowing gently at the smouldering dust, he heaved a sigh of relief as the red glow burst into yellow, consuming flames. He built a good fire and wrapped a cloth around the shaman. He was still asleep.

Red Horse decided to look around the cavern. It was quite large and very dark in its interior spaces. Taking a torch from the fire he investigated the cavern and soon found what he took to be the shaman's sleeping quarters.

There was a bed of skins laid out and Red Horse thought it best to put the shaman on them. It was presumably here that he wanted to die. Having positioned Tolmec on the bed, he cleaned his seeping wound. The shaman was as still as death as Red Horse covered his body with more skins. Red Horse's chattering teeth betrayed the fact that he was feeling the cold – and therefore, that the effect of the herbs had diminished. He moved closer to the fire, tugging a blanket tightly around his hunched shoulders. As he did so, he watched in quiet fascination as the hair on his arms began to fall out in tufts.

As an Osage he was used to going without food, but he could not resist the temptation to descend further into the valley to see if it was as promising a hunting ground as it appeared to be from a distance. He decided there was little else he could do for the shaman. In any case, he needed to build up his own strength if he was to descend from the mountain to find Neli again.

He spent what remained of the day scouting around the lower reaches of the valley. He saw no sign of human habitation, but there was plenty of evidence of animal life; never before had he seen so many different creatures grazing together. There was food aplenty.

He returned to the cavern to find Tolmec awake. Nevertheless, the medicine man would only accept a little hot broth.

Red Horse fed him slowly and enquired: "Tolmec, I would like to know more of this place. How long have you had an encampment here?

"Can you remember how many times our brother the moon has flooded the land at night with his brightness? Or how many times the clouds have burst, and shed their tears?" The Osage warrior shrugged his shoulders.

"Forgive an old man, my son. I do not know the answer to your question! I have not counted the years. My woman and I were born here, in the valley. There was a time when my people lived here and we knew nothing of wars and envy. But some of us found a way out of the valley and went down to the plains beyond the mountains. A small number returned with tales of splendour and riches – most never returned at all. We had everything we could want here, but men are always curious and the allure of the outside world was strong. Few could resist the temptation to see the world beyond and as time passed, more and more of our people deserted the valley. Then came a time when we had no elders left. They had all, one by one, gone down to the plains outside and not returned. It seemed to us that life outside the valley must be wonderful, for most of those who waved goodbye chose not to come back. So, one day, my woman and I decided to leave. By then, we had been together for twenty winters, from birth!"

Red Horse offered Tolmec more broth; shaking his head, he refused.

"It would be hard for you to imagine how strange and exciting we found the outside. We had heard many tales of the people who roamed the land and we thought we knew what to expect. But we hid in fear when we saw pale-faced horsemen chasing a man whose skin was as black as night. From our hiding place we watched, mesmerized, as they hung him from a tall tree."

Red Horse offered Tolmec a clay jar containing water. The shaman sipped a little and then continued: "We were appalled at such savagery. We returned to the valley and did not leave it again for many days. But like bees passing a honeysuckle flower, the lure of the outside was too strong. It is good to learn about the world and to extend one's knowledge of all things; but there are dangers!"

Beneath the mound of skins, Tolmec went silent. Red Horse waited patiently for him to resume the tale. Suddenly, the old man's eyes opened again: "On our second trip outside, a hunter stumbled upon us as we were drinking from a stream. We fled, but as we made our escape, he shot my woman."

He coughed roughly in an attempt to clear his throat,

his breathing now phlegmatic: "Hidden in the brush I watched the hunter attack her body with his skinning knife. He hung my woman's head from the horn of his saddle. Not satisfied with this atrocity, he attacked her body again." The painful memory was too much for Tolmec to dwell on and he closed his eyes for a moment.

"She was heavy with child," he said, leaning forward, the old grief gripping him again. "When she died, the strong medicine of the herbs began to lose its hold on her body, and in a short time she was once again restored to herself. As the hair fell out and her body shrank to its normal size the white man began to curse his god again and again, before mounting his horse."

"What did you do?" demanded Red Horse.

Struggling to sit upright, Tolmec's eyes stared at Red Horse with an unseeing gaze: "Crazy with my loss, I charged at him; I cared not whether I lived or died. I pulled the white man from his horse and beat him about the head until he lay senseless before me. I could have killed him then. My thought was to smash his skull with a boulder. But as I raised my arms, I caught sight of my woman's body. I was overcome by grief and collapsed. After some time, I dug a grave and buried her remains within it. Then I walked away, carrying her memory with me. I carry it still." He fell back with exhaustion, trembling slightly.

Red Horse drew the blanket under his chin. "Rest, shaman, be at peace. She waits for you with the spirits of your ancestors. You will see her again, be sure!"

Red Horse left the shaman for a few moments to give the old man time to compose himself. He wandered around the cavern examining the drawings on the walls. His nostrils flared on detecting an unpleasant, acrid smell emanating from a corner of the cave – a strong smell of urine. 'Is this the shaman's latrine?' he wondered. It seemed strange, for Indians were meticulous in such arrangements and latrine areas were always outside a cave or tent. As he walked in the darkness Red Horse's feet began to crunch on discarded bones lying in the passageway.

So this cavern had been the shaman's retreat since he was a young man? He looked at Tolmec's few possessions, the accumulated riches of fifty years: there was a bow and some arrows; the skins he was lying upon and a large tobacco pipe. Violent coughing made him hurry back to the shaman's side; he was awake again. Examining the old man's wound, Red Horse said: "Your blood runs again, Tolmec."

"Huh, it shows I am still alive - when it stops, I will be no more."

"Why did you not kill the white man?"

"I did, my son. I decided his death would not be quick or crude - subtlety was called for." Tolmec pointed at his smoking pipe with great effort, his arm flopping down across his body. Quickly, Red Horse filled the pipe and placed it in Tolmec's hands. He then touched the tobacco with a smouldering twig. The old man drew deeply on the pipe and the bowl glowed red. He released the pungent smoke through his lips and when he spoke again his voice was a feeble croak. Red Horse leaned closer to hear him.

"I prayed to the Great Spirit, then ate the special herbs. I came down from the mountain and tracked the man back to his camp. He was easy to find - he lived just outside the white man's village." Red Horse slipped an arm around Tolmec's shoulder as his face turned ashen. "Faces from the distant past beckon to me…"

Filled with curiosity, Red Horse urged the dying man to finish.

"For two moons I appeared before the white man. Sometimes I would stare at him from a distance before walking away into some trees; at other times I would wander past his camp at night as he sat by his fire. I made sure he saw me, but no one else; the creature he had first seen drinking from the stream had come back to haunt him! He must have guessed I sought vengeance and I wanted him to know fear. No doubt his friends thought he was going mad. I heard them laughing at him as he tried to describe the wild man who followed him. But he had no evidence to show I even existed. Then, one night, as I stared at him from the brushwood, he looked back at me. I saw him grip the barrel of a gun between his teeth and pull the trigger… I had killed him without laying a hand upon him… I was satisfied – but bitter at what had befallen me."

Red Horse chose to change the subject to staunch the old man's tears.

"What is the strange scent that fills the air of your lodge?" he enquired.

Tolmec beckoned him to come closer, his voice now just a whisper: "Beware of the guardian, it is…"

The blood from his wound had stopped flowing. Slowly, Red Horse placed the smoking pipe across the shaman's chest.

He looked at the lifeless body, one question in his mind: *"What did Tolmec mean by 'guardian'?"*

He looked towards the dark recesses of the cavern and piled more wood onto the dying fire. Now he remembered what the scent reminded him of – it was the spoor of a puma, a big mountain cat. Nervously, Red

Horse gripped his hunting knife and waited for the first light of day...

"You have been fire dreaming, old man! Your snoring has frightened the children!" Red Horse came back to reality with a nudge from his wife, Neli, that startled him. The others laughed as she scolded him. Neli smiled and touched his arm affectionately. "Listen to RoShann," she whispered.

RoShann faced them squarely and began politely: "I, Roshann of the Sasquatchoni, would like to thank my Osage brothers – and sisters - for their many gifts and hospitality. I am indebted to you and must in honour repay your favours. There is little I can do now other than to offer you my labour. If it pleases you, I would like to help you build your family a lodge, of the same kind that houses the Sasquatchoni!"

Red Horse was delighted with the proposition. He had always admired the permanent structure and village layout of the Sasquatchoni encampments.

Then Neli spoke: "Come, Concilla, we have much to do. We shall select the position."

Early in the morning the two warriors worked hard to select, cut and trim all the wood they would need for the frame of the dwelling. Neli and Concilla, with help from the children, cleared the chosen site for the lodge.

With impish enjoyment, the children managed to collect bundles of reeds at the river's edge, sufficient for the nimble fingers of the women to plait and weave into lining mats for the roof and sides of the house.

Now, with the hard toil of the physical work behind them, the last hole dug and several logs placed in upright positions, both warriors rested, pleased with the progress they had made. As the days passed, the lodge gradually took shape, and RoShann led the task of covering the last of the reed walls with layers of river mud. When it was finished, the excited women moved quickly through the doorway of the lodge to lay more reed mats down as a floor covering and, within moments, had started their cooking fire. They watched in fascination as a small flame gave way to a billowing cloud of smoke that hung lazily on the rafters - then, like a huge rattlesnake, the head of the plume weaved from side to side as if searching for the smoke hole; when it found the exit it seemed to hesitate for a second, before gathering up its body to strike the flue. At last, the draught drew it through, leaving the flames dancing high.

RoShann listened to the women laughing and singing as they began preparing a meal. They feasted well in celebration of the completion of the new lodge.

"I am content with your gift, RoShann," said Red Horse. "For one so young, you have much skill and wisdom."

RoShann was gratified by the compliment, replying: "Did the Great Spirit not command us to pass on our knowledge to our brothers, so that they can benefit?"

"Yes, that is the way of the Osage tribe," answered Red Horse. He fell silent for a few moments, as if struggling with a decision. Finally, he said:

"In the morning, when you are ready, I will show you around the valley."

* * * *

"The Great Spirit has been good to you!" cried RoShann, as he surveyed the beauty of the surrounding landscape. Red Horse chuckled at the younger man's wonderment.

They watched silently as a skein of geese headed north, honking and cooing to each other till the entire flock landed on the lake. Some of the fowl made for the shore and immediately started their search for wild corn, while others were happy to rest upon the waters preening their ruffled feathers.

"A warrior could never go hungry here!" commented RoShann with a smile at Red Horse. "You have a rich hunting ground here, my friend, and I envy you. Yet still you have not told me the tale of how you found this land. Will you do so now?"

Red Horse gazed at the snow-covered mountains surrounding the valley and at the tallest peak that marked out their destination. The tranquillity of the place affected them both and they felt compelled to relax for a while to admire the view. RoShann stretched out full length alongside the lake with his arms cupped behind his neck, as Red Horse squatted on his haunches and related his strange story.

Brushing away the mosquitoes as he listened, RoShann found the Osage warrior's account hard to believe. He made a silent decision to question the girl Concilla about the extraordinary details, when he was next alone with her. He liked Red Horse and afforded him great respect, but he began to consider that perhaps two long winters in the valley had affected his mind. The story was just too difficult to accept without further questioning. Surely, it was a fantasy?

'So an old shaman led Red Horse here? And Red Horse was able to traverse the snow thanks to peculiar herbs that could change a man's body? Bah! The Osage is playing games with me!'

Red Horse noticed the skeptical look on the young Sasquatchoni's face, but was not offended. Touching RoShann's shoulder he said, "Come."

He walked away, leaving RoShann to catch up.

It was easy enough to follow the Osage warrior's tracks through the springy grass and into the forest, past the fallen hulks of old pine trees and on though a dense thicket of scrubland. Entering a clearing, he followed the tracks up an incline and found Red Horse waiting. Without speaking, the Osage pointed upwards at the towering mountain. RoShann trod carefully along the same path as the older man and watched with admiration as Red Horse climbed, jumped and clawed his way higher. Eventually, they reached their objective: a worn track leading to a cave entrance. Red Horse threw himself down on the ground to rest his aching body. RoShann went to relieve himself against a tall pine tree, but instead, bent down and sniffed around its base. The scent was unmistakable. When he had finished he returned to the Osage.

"The cavern is the den of a mountain lion."

"I know," answered Red Horse blankly.

'Is this to be a final test of my courage?' thought RoShann. The Osage must have known of the big cat's presence, yet he had said nothing. RoShann knew that pumas were

solitary in nature and rarely attacked humans without provocation. His respect for living things would not allow him to take its life without good cause; the regard of one hunter for another was ingrained in him.

"I would deem it an honour if you would allow me to demonstrate how a Sasquatchoni would deal with our sister, the cat!"

Red Horse was genuinely curious to see how the young warrior would tackle the problem and he nodded his assent to RoShann.

RoShann searched the nearby pine trees for a stout six-foot branch. Having found a suitable example, he cut it down and trimmed it smooth, leaving a fork of smaller branches at the end. Then, with extreme caution, both warriors approached the cavern entrance. RoShann looked down at the steep drop behind him and chose a place to stand. He motioned to Red Horse, who immediately picked up some pebbles and threw them forcefully into the cavern whilst emitting a loud war cry.

Standing like a defensive boxer, RoShann took up his position with the fork of the branch touching the ground. He tightened his grip on the stock in expectation of what was to follow. Soon, the gleaming yellow eyes of the puma showed in the depths of the cavern. It was clear the animal was advancing. Snarling and hissing, the female cat launched her tawny colored body directly at RoShann. She flew through the air with a blood-curdling snarl, her claws bared. RoShann uttered a prayer to the Great Spirit 'Manitou', as he quickly jerked the forked branch upright, hooking the puma beneath her front shoulders. Her momentum and RoShann's great strength did the rest: the mountain lion was propelled over his head, twisting and turning as it fell, before crashing noisily through a willow tree fifty feet below. Its descent through the slender catkins caused a shower of fluffy yellow flowers to fall. Desperately, the puma dug her claws into the branches as she slithered to the ground.

Shaking and licking herself, she ran off in terror.

"It won't come back. It will remember the shock it suffered here!" averred RoShann.

Together, the two men entered the cavern.

After lighting a fire RoShann was able to examine the mysterious drawings on the walls. Artful depictions of men and animals were interspersed with arcane symbols in many colors. He stared at them thoughtfully: "These pictures are old. Many winters have passed since these hunters lived here."

Red Horse nodded his head in agreement.

"I have never seen beasts such as this!" remarked

RoShann. He stepped back a couple of paces to try to understand the scale and proportion of the prehistoric animals the artist had painted.

Red Horse began making some torches, rubbing them liberally with a supply of fat he had brought from his lodge. He gestured at the inky darkness of the cavern beyond the firelight.

"That is where the old shaman lived and died," he said. His voice was muted and hollow. "Now we must go up to the snow line to gather some herbs."

They went outside into the daylight and found that a mist had drifted down from the higher reaches of the mountainside. Red Horse tilted his head back and half closed his eyes in an attempt to see a familiar landmark.

Without looking at RoShann, he said: "Up there! That is the only way out."

As was the way with all Indians, RoShann had been taught from an early age to recognize which herbs were good to eat and which were not. The Great Spirit had made them all available for different reasons; those that were of no use to man, were of use to some other creature. But he did not recognize the root plucked from the cold soil by Red Horse; he was perplexed by its thin, elongated shape and speckled appearance. It did not look appetizing.

Nevertheless, Red Horse asked him to look for more and when they had found a small quantity they returned, once again, to the cavern.

Red Horse plunged his newly made torches into the fire. When they were burning properly, he led the way to the old shaman's burial chamber.

RoShann stared intently at the bones of the medicine man and felt that Red Horse had begun to redeem himself. Clearly, he had spoken the truth; there was a cavern and there had been a shaman living within it. But how could a simple herb change the appearance of a man's body? Such powerful medicine was unknown to the plains tribes.

A dense cascade of stalactites festooning the roof of the cavern attracted RoShann's attention. He examined them closely, fascinated by their smooth perfection. The light of the torches reflected off their polished surfaces and emphasized their rich pink hue. It also revealed a labyrinth of tunnels leading off from the main chamber.

"I have explored some of those passages," said Red Horse. "They are like this place, but with the pointed rocks growing from the ground. Come, before the light fades." He lit the spare torch and handed it to RoShann. Then they began to make their way back along the twisting corridor.

The two men sat around the blazing fire, grateful that

it dispelled the shadows and coolness of the dying day. Red Horse handed RoShann his share of the unfamiliar herbs.

"Eat!" he said, as he began vigorously chewing his own portion.

RoShann felt foolish in complying with Red Horse's wish because he did not believe that a mere herb could change a man's body. But the fierce unblinking eyes of the Osage warrior threw out their silent challenge. He disliked the bitter flavour of the plant and wanted to retch, but he controlled his reflexes; he would not allow himself to lose face. He swallowed the last of the fibrous roots with a gulp of water.

For a short time nothing happened. Then his bloodstream started to absorb the herb's natural substances. Under their influence he began to hallucinate. He sat with his eyes closed, not wanting to move; RoShann was afraid he would drown in the bizarre floating sensations he was experiencing. Clamping both hands to his face he tried to steady his whirling senses; a muffled groan escaped from his clenched jaw. Wet with perspiration, he was aware of fine hair growing on his face as he dragged his fingers down to his chest. The heat generated by his body was overwhelming. He threw off his blanket and moved away from the fire.

Red Horse spoke from the shadows.

"Do you not agree, it is a powerful medicine?" Without waiting for a reply he stepped forward into the orange light. "Look! We are the same!"

RoShann examined himself and then looked at the Osage. Red Horse was no longer a normal man. He had become part animal, part human – or so it seemed. He had grown a thick coat of reddish brown hair, just like the mane that now completely covered RoShann's body.

"Not a single member of your tribe would know you now, Sasquatchoni warrior!" commented Red Horse. "But we must hurry - let us climb through the snow."

The two men found climbing the mountain exhilarating. The cold, thin air was no impediment to their strengthened lungs and the increased rate of their blood circulation kept them warm. They ploughed on through the snow, carving a zig-zag trail amongst the drifts.

"RoShann, I must rest!" protested a weary Red Horse to the energetic young warrior. "Will you run all the way back to your father's lodge?"

They stopped to recuperate and watched in amusement as clouds of steam rose in the chilled air from the heat of their bodies.

"We are two grown men, and yet we play like children witnessing their first snowfall!" smiled RoShann. They hurled snow at each other, laughing at the absurdity of their game, before resting once more. With a serious tone to his voice, Red Horse advised RoShann:

"When your body begins to feel the cold winds, it will start to lose its fur and you will quickly become yourself again."

RoShann remembered well the previous winter - when it was so cold the people of his tribe had wrapped themselves in bundles of old rags in their vain attempts to keep warm. Only the hunters had gone out, some never to return, as the worst blizzards in living memory blew across the plains.

"Do you shake your head in disbelief?" enquired Red Horse.

"No, my brother. I feel sorrow for events of the past. This valley is now as the prairies once were. There are no white men here, only Indian tribesmen. This is as it was - when our ancestors roamed these lands."

A strong gust of wind came howling through the valley pitching showers of snowflakes at them as it danced along the mountain peaks.

"I think the spirit of the old shaman is still with us," said RoShann.

Red Horse nodded. "Let us make our way back to the fire."

THE SECRET VALLEY

* * * *

Concilla finished tacking the last piece of colored cloth to the buckskin shirt with small, neat stitches. Pleased with her work, she folded the pants and shirt together, her thoughts full of RoShann.

Whilst completing the task, her mind had wandered over the past and the possibilities for her future. She reflected that it might have been better if she had stayed with the Osage elders and their families in the reservation. There, she would have had the company of friends and people of her own age… When darkness fell in the valley she was often disturbed by the stifled sounds of Red Horse and Neli as they coupled. Red Horse had always treated her correctly, but she had noticed that the Osage warrior was becoming more aware of her womanly charms. Occasionally, as she searched for wild cabbage or herbs she would glance up and catch him watching her. She knew the reason for his interest. In the Osage tribe there had always been more women than men; some warriors had three or four wives and many children. Although it was an accepted custom, she did not want to live her life in that way.

Her thoughts were interrupted by the exuberant cries of the children:

"They come, Red Horse and RoShann!"

As the young ones went racing off to meet the men, Neli touched Concilla's arm to indicate that they should wait outside the lodge.

The two warriors arrived with the children laughing merrily. Red Horse swung his young son down off his back. The giant Sasquatchoni bent down carefully and lowered the two girls so they could find their feet. As he stood upright again he found the youngest child had clung onto him; she had her arms locked tightly around his neck.

Concilla held the child and gently tickled her ribs. Laughing and crying at the same time, the child fell into her arms. "You have made a conquest, RoShann," she said.

"I would much prefer it to be you," he replied. "You are more my size!" He smiled at her and moved across to greet Neli.

Concilla felt a sudden rush of blood to her face at his avowal and all that it implied. Nevertheless, the remark gave her a wonderful feeling of elation. Hugging the child to her breast she smothered its soft flesh with kisses.

The following few days were happy and peaceful for the two young people. They began spending more time in each other's company, exchanging views and stories about their tribes and families.

As he hunted for food near the lake, RoShann was absorbed by considerations of nature, tradition, and rites. He remembered his father telling him that just as the cold earth awaited the first rays of the morning sun to provide warmth, so should a young brave await the light and warmth of a woman. *The green land rises up to meet the sun and flourishes in its presence - so it is, between a man and a woman.*

He cut a small bush loose and entered the water, pushing the shrub in front of him as he swam. Concealed behind the twiggy screen, he eased his way towards the waterfowl. Most of the geese were feeding, some filling their gizzards with small pebbles. As he neared them, he quickly submerged and grabbed the feet of the nearest bird. The goose tried to fly away - but with a swift movement he expertly broke its neck, and struck out for the shore. He splashed out of the water and threw the dead goose on the grass, then sat down to rest in the warm noonday sun. With his eyes closed he thought about his family, the change in his appearance when he ate the magical roots - and about Concilla.

"Ah," he smiled to himself, straightening his breechcloth. "She's the one that makes my body change – almost as much as the herbs."

A sudden chorus of honking geese startled him.

Beating their wings frantically, they sounded their alarm calls and rose quickly into the air with much agitation. RoShann was puzzled.

'What could have frightened them?' he wondered.

"RoShann!"

He spun around at the sound of his name.

"Concilla!"

She waved at him from the lake shallows. RoShann waded out into the water to help her reach the shore. As she struggled to stand in the soft mud of the lake floor she held out her arms, inviting him to steady her.

RoShann advanced, but then paused - he could do nothing but stare. The wet clothing clung to Concilla's body like a second skin. It enhanced her figure enticingly, moulding itself around her breasts and emphasizing the curve of her hips.

Neither knew or cared how it happened; their arms entwined as they kissed fiercely, hungrily. Obeying a natural impulse they lay down in the long grass, touching and caressing each other gently.

Paying due respect to Red Horse and Neli, RoShann advised them of his intentions regarding a pairing with Concilla and asked that they should bless the union. Red Horse regretted that she came with no dowry, but

RoShann waived the issue aside:

"That is of no concern to me," he said. "I am very glad to have found such a woman. We live in difficult times, Red Horse. Now we shall truly be brothers!"

Alone with each other later on, the two sisters conferred about the relationship.

"You are a woman now, Concilla?" enquired Neli. Her lips were pressed hard together as she tried to stop her smile from spreading.

Concilla held up four fingers.

"In one day, I'm a woman this many times!"

Neli drew in a breath and rolled her eyes. "Now you are one of us!" she said.

Laughing happily, they continued with their work.

For a while thereafter the young couple lived an idyllic existence, lustfully making love whenever the urge came upon them. After the passing of several full moons they began to construct a new lodge, where they could set up home together. But Concilla sensed that RoShann was restless and still desired to leave the valley. The psychic bond between them had become too powerful for her not to notice his disquiet. One day, she confronted him with her perceptions.

"When will you go?" she asked earnestly.

"Does my face tell everyone its secrets?" he replied.

"Yes," said Concilla, moving closer. "Every day you look at the mountains, but you see beyond them!"

RoShann placed his arms around her waist and together they gazed at the sunset as it silhouetted the mountains. The noise of the chirruping crickets seemed only to accentuate the hushed solitude of the evening.

She continued to express her anguish: "Is it not a beautiful land, my husband? Are you so unhappy?"

He looked at her affectionately and gave her the explanation she sought:

"Concilla, we have known each other for only a short time, yet you read my thoughts like an open trail. Yes, the valley is beautiful and you have brought joy into my life. But I have blood ties elsewhere. My family and tribe do not know where I am, or what happened to me. I worry about them, as I am sure they worry about me. I need to know they are well. I cannot stay here much longer."

They walked a few steps together as RoShann struggled to rationalize his feelings. In a thoughtful mood, he spoke again:

"Now, I understand why the shaman and his people wandered the prairie. No Indian can stay in one place for long, lest he strike roots and become anchored to the spot like a tree!"

In a flat tone, Concilla said simply, "When?"

"In two days," said RoShann, "- and as my wife, you shall accompany me. We will use the herbs to follow the trail over the mountains. Oh, and… if you spot an eagle's nest as we climb, please tell me. I want to collect some feathers…"

5. A SOLDIER'S PRIDE

Colonel Henry Cornwell Austin was a man of slight stature and large ambitions. He had managed to survive the destructive rigors of the Civil War without a scratch and although battle honors had somehow eluded him he remained proud of his service. He was determined to make an impact in his new position as commanding officer of Fort Kearny. Despite some occasional frustrations with his role he always retained an opportunistic eye for the advancement of his military career.

As he traced out the route of the seventh cavalry with a fingertip he gazed distractedly at the crossed regimental colors pinned to the wall and stroked the bristles on his chin.

"That glory seeking sonofabitch, Custer! He must of had the ear of someone in Washington!" he asserted.

"Yeah, that's what it was! Our hero bit off more than he could chew that day, that's for sure!"

Looking at the killing ground of the Little Big Horn, he shook his head with disbelief and slapped the wall map in disgust.

"That vainglorious fool! I'd have approached the situation with entirely different tactics."

His jaw jutted out defiantly as he considered the resolve needed when dealing with savage tribes. He decided that from now on he would no longer attend council meetings with the Indian chiefs. He would leave that tiresome chore to Major Timothy O'Hara, who apparently thought so highly of them. But at the first sign of any trouble he would ruthlessly force them to concede.

"Damn it! History will remember Henry Cornwell Austin!"

With his hands pressed together in an attitude of prayer he touched his bottom lip and stepped forward a few paces, as the germ of an idea entered his mind.

"I could always say, I wasn't kept informed by my second officer!" He smiled contentedly at the pleasurable thought. He was so absorbed in his cogitations that a sudden knock on the door startled him.

"Come!" He looked towards the door expectantly. It was O'Hara.

"What is it, major?" he enquired irritably. He found it difficult to control his antagonism towards O'Hara and did not acknowledge his salute. Whenever he saw the major he was reminded of the time when he had listened to an itinerant preacher as a child. The preacher had said: *'If you think hard enough about the devil, he will appear before your eyes.'*

"There's a deputation of chiefs from the Sasquatchoni tribe outside, and they demand that you speak with them - sir." O'Hara accentuated the last word.

Colonel Austin's tight-ridged jaw muscles relaxed slowly as his hands gradually uncurled from behind his back. "Very well, major, I shall do so. But remember my orders: No Indians are to be allowed to enter the confines of the fort."

O'Hara watched with unblinking eyes as an emotional struggle took place within Colonel Austin and made itself visible on his face. The colonel was affronted by both O'Hara's manner and the Indians' impudence. His thoughts raced along their customary track:

'So, they demand to see me do they? I was under the impression that it was the dog that wagged its tail!'

He recovered his composure and made a decision. In a sneering voice laden with sarcasm he said: "On the other hand, major, perhaps it is time to build bridges with the Indians? I know it's something you are personally keen on.

All right - I'll break the rules this time. Let our Indian 'brothers' enter the fort."

"Somehow, I thought you would, colonel!"

Grabbing his hat the colonel went outside and waited impatiently on the verandah steps where he was to receive the Indian delegates. The location was chosen to ensure that the visitors would have to look up to him. Throughout his adult life he had often felt intimidated by taller men. His inferiority complex had caused some difficulties during his career, but the sight of the Sasquatchoni warriors advancing towards him made his stomach muscles contract involuntarily. Fighting to control his distaste, he held his ground.

Of the many prairie tribes Colonel Austin had encountered over the years he considered the Sasquatchoni warriors to be the most magnificently attired. They had great skill in working leather and bone and made much use of colorful dyes to decorate their garments. They had originally been a hunting and horse breeding people, but they had adapted their way of life to the modern era and were now traders and farmers. They were an industrious people, quick to learn new tricks and had recently laid claim to a vast area of fertile land as their ancestral hunting ground. Colonel Austin harbored a keen resentment towards the Sasquatchoni - not least because the army had been required to obtain the tribe's permission to build Fort Kearny. He summed up his antipathy in a phrase he would repeat to anyone who would listen: *'Those big-assed bastards have got way too much of everything!'*

At the approach of the delegation the colonel did no more than touch his hat above the right eye in a desultory gesture of acknowledgement. The Sasquatchoni made their formal salutations of respect and then Tonala, their chief, prodded his horse forward. Without dismounting, his formidable frame leaned forward and he looked straight into Colonel Austin's eyes.

"My scouts report seeing many white hunters in the Black Hills, together with men who search for gold. For the Indian, that is sacred land and must not be violated. The hills are the resting place of the Great Spirit Manitou!"

Tonala paused to let his words sink into the minds of his audience. His physical stature and imposing bearing commanded the attention of all those present.

He continued in a firm voice: "We signed a peace treaty with your army. Your chiefs agreed to protect our lands." Waving his lance, Tonala pointed it in different directions: "More and more white men invade our territory. They come like vultures, to pick it clean and leave only the bones. Why are they allowed to do this? Is the white man's word meaningless?"

Colonel Austin listened uncomfortably to the Indian's charges and attempted to rebut his condemnatory address:

"Your words are strong, Tonala - and they are sharp. Though I may not bleed, they wound me. If my land had been invaded I, too, would be angry. I can assure you that army patrols have turned back hundreds of prospectors - but my men can't be everywhere! I'm sure Tonala understands the situation." Colonel Austin gripped the verandah rail tightly with both hands. Tonala observed the man's knuckles whitening, even as his face smiled.

"I'll make this promise to you, Tonala: the army will increase its patrols of the Black Hills, and if we find any prospectors - why, every man jack o'them will be sent packing!"

Tonala turned to his companions to explain Colonel Austin's new pledge in their own language. Then, for Austin's benefit, he spent several minutes detailing the precise boundary lines and waypoints that defined Indian territory in the Black Hills. Having secured assurances from Colonel Austin that the boundaries would be respected Tonala turned to leave, taking his escort of Sasquatchoni warriors with him.

Colonel Austin smiled until the last Sasquatchoni had passed through the big gates; when they had all gone, he exploded with anger. "Major!" - he bellowed the word as he strode the short distance to his quarters. His second-in-command had not yet appeared, so with one last shout of 'major!' the colonel swung the command post door open, walked in and slammed it shut.

O'Hara trudged towards the office with his teeth clenched firmly together. He braced himself for the confrontation that would surely follow. Without bothering to knock, he leaned against the colonel's door and walked in.

"You wanted to see me, colonel?"

The colonel was pacing around the room in an agitated manner: "Damn right I wanted to see you, mister! I take it you heard those impudent bastards!"

Colonel Austin ground the words out in hot-blooded anger, unable to hide his indignation.

"Those insolent red skinned curs; they talk to me as though I'm a… a mere errand boy – me!" His balled fist crashed down on the leather topped desk, scattering a desk manifold.

"Don't they know I'm a colonel in the United States Army?" He jabbed at his chest with a stiff finger. "Do they even know what that means? Well, if they don't, then they're sure gonna learn." Pouring himself a shot of whiskey he threw it to the back of his throat. "I'll bet they're laughing at me all the way back to their lodges! Oh yes! Can't you just hear it, major? *Look at the way we ordered the white man around. He has to do what we say. We made him look a fool!*"

O'Hara protested vigorously: "That's unfair, sir, and you know it. I think you're reading things into it that aren't there. The Sasquatchoni accorded you all due respect as commander of Fort Kearny. They just want us to keep our side of the bargain."

"Oh, really? You think so? Well, I'm grateful for your advice, major, even though it entirely misses the point. Now listen to me! I'm posting orders banning all Indians from this fort until further notice! They are to be stopped at the gate and turned away - and if they refuse to leave they are to be encouraged to do so by the use of rifle shots. And that applies particularly to the Sasquatchoni - those overgrown motherfucking sons of red bitches! There will be no more negotiations with savages and no more safeguarding of Indian 'rights'!"

"Colonel, if I may speak freely - you're making a big mistake," said O'Hara. "We can't go back to the old way of dealing with the Indians. Times have changed. We've all got an interest in maintaining the peace. There are white landholders out there who won't thank you for stoking up unrest amongst the tribes and adding to their grievances. If our men treat the Sasquatchoni with contempt - if you break your word - we'll have trouble on our hands. The Cheyenne, the Sioux and the Shoshone will back them all the way."

"I'm pulling all patrols back, major. I don't see why we should waste valuable time and soldiers patrolling areas that are precious only to a bunch of heathens."

Colonel Austin's attitude surprised O'Hara. "You can't be serious? The hills are part of their ancestral homeland – the home of their gods. What is it with you colonel? This isn't about the Sasquatchoni. It's about you stirring up trouble with the Indians so you can crush a rebellion and gain some medals. That's it, isn't it? You don't care about the lives of ordinary people here and how they might be affected - just so long as you get a nice polished desk and a senior command position." The tone of O'Hara's voice reflected his disgust that Austin should seek to stir up old hatreds in such a manner. "Don't you make any distinction between Indians?"

"I'm quite aware of all the relevant facts, major," snapped the colonel testily. "My primary duty is to protect the civilized white community, not the hostiles!"

"You are so damn wrong, don't you see that?"

"Major, all I want from you is a new duty roster. Please see that my orders are carried out."

The bad blood between the two was volatile. O'Hara saluted and turned to leave. As he opened the door, he stopped.

"Would you answer me one question?"

Colonel Austin raised his eyebrows, but did not demur.

"How the hell did you get to be an officer!"

Without waiting for the colonel's reply, O'Hara stalked out letting the heavy door close itself with a thud.

The following morning, Colonel Austin was still smarting from the previous day's exchanges.

He considered O'Hara to be grossly insubordinate and in need of correctional training. He had long ago formed the view that an appropriate military attitude could only be instilled by means of discipline and hardship. With that thought in mind, the colonel decided that O'Hara should be put in charge of a hanging detail. It would be a subtle form of punishment considering how much he disliked that form of execution - especially if the prisoner happened to be an Indian.

If nothing else, it would teach him the realities that had to be faced if white people were to share the land with Indians...

SASQUATCH MAN

* * * *

The small town of Faber's Creek was bursting at the seams with people: hunters, prospectors, prostitutes and carpetbaggers; a whole multitude of derelicts, many of whom spent their entire lives wandering hopefully from one town to another, chasing their luck. Along the town's main street they rubbed shoulders with other itinerants: homesteaders, ranchers, cattle drovers and casual laborers. They had all prospered at the expense of the Arapaho tribe, once the dominant force in the region. The tribe's chief, Masekala, had innocently given up all claim to the title deeds of the surrounding land; he did not understand the concept of land ownership, nor the idea that such a thing could be conferred by a piece of paper in a lawyer's office.

O'Hara dismissed his escorting troop and went to see the town's marshal. The local lawman was a thickset individual with a pockmarked, weather-beaten face. He greeted O'Hara solicitously:

"Howdy, major - you ready for the fireworks?"

"Well, I hope there won't be any, Tom - we're just here to keep the peace. I understand there's quite a few prospectors in town."

"Yeah, it's getting to be more like a carnival every

day. They seem to think that just 'cause old Faber once found gold here, there's a chance that maybe - just maybe - there could still be a pocketful of paydirt lying around somewhere!"

"Time will tell," smiled O'Hara. "I'd better check on Chief Masekala."

He opened the door leading to the interior of the cellblock as the marshal described the situation.

"Ah, well - he says he won't die by hanging, major. Since the trial two days ago, he hasn't eaten a thing! I told him you might want to talk to him, before justice is done."

O'Hara walked down the short corridor and stopped opposite the chief's cell. The Indian was sitting cross-legged on the floor, seemingly oblivious to the presence of his visitor. O'Hara cleared his throat and addressed the condemned man directly: "Masekala!'

The chief broke from his trance and looked up. He rose and approached the iron bars to stare at O'Hara. For a few seconds neither man spoke as each assessed the other's appearance. Then Masekala said in his own tongue: "Major - can you give me freedom?"

Without waiting for O'Hara's reply he continued: "Of course not; I do not need your answer. The white man only takes possessions; he never gives them back." A guttural tone in his voice betrayed his bitterness.

O'Hara ignored the barb and tried again: "Masekala, I'm told that shortly after you left the reservation your men killed a homesteader and his family. Is that true?"

Masekala stiffened and looked into O'Hara's eyes. "The army killed seven of my warriors and has now condemned me to death by hanging." His emotionless brown eyes offered neither justification nor repentance. He continued coldly: "There are always casualties in wars."

"But we are not at war," countered O'Hara.

"Are we not? Since the first white man trod these lands my people have known nothing but war - along with grief and hatred."

O'Hara looked at the stony face of the Indian.

"I'm sorry you feel that way, Masekala. Then I'm afraid there is nothing I can do."

"So be it, major. I shall die like a warrior of the Arapaho!"

Masekala turned his back on O'Hara and settled himself down on the dirt floor in his former position. He threw a blanket loosely around his shoulders as the major made his exit. He heard a key being turned in the lock and the sound of spurred footsteps receding behind the adjoining door.

When all was quiet once more, Masekala focused his attention on the cell's small, iron-barred window. Beyond it were gray thunderclouds and a blue sky; a sure sign of approaching rain. As he watched the clouds pass by, Masekala withdrew into himself and settled his mind. He accepted that his life was soon to end – all that remained for him to do was to pray to his ancestors and to the Great Spirit.

Strangely, as the hour of his execution drew ever nearer he felt his senses becoming more acute than at any other time in his life. He concentrated so intensely on the floating clouds that it seemed as though the iron bars of the window had disappeared; it was a pleasing illusion and he did not blink for fear of breaking its spell. As slanting sunbeams streaked through the window he observed flies dancing lazily in their warmth; particles of dust were drifting aimlessly in the golden rays and a spider was busily refurbishing its web with delicate silk-like threads.

After some time meditating, Masekala gradually allowed his strained neck muscles to relax. He lowered his head and blinked two or three times. He watched idly as small beetles scurried over the portion of greasy food on his tin plate. It was of no concern: he would never eat again.

Somewhere in the distance he could hear a bull bellowing in the cattle pens. The sound brought back memories of his youth: a time when he and other young warriors had recklessly chased buffalo across the plains.

O'Hara had long since departed, but Masekala looked around to make sure he was alone. Then he pulled himself up to the iron-barred window. He could hear the Arapaho drums and he felt comforted by their timbre; the tribe was chanting his death song.

The noisy crowd was held back by the presence of the troopers, each soldier standing an arm's length from his fellows.

A voice shouted out from the midst of the throng: "Here comes the marshal! Twelve noon and dead on time!'

The marshal pushed his watch deep into his waistcoat pocket and noted with stern satisfaction that the spectators seemed intent on behaving themselves. He beckoned to the men in the jail to come out.

Flanked on each side by a deputy, with his hands manacled behind his back, Masekala walked alone to the accompaniment of the Arapaho drums. As he moved through the corridor of troopers, his eyes glanced fleetingly at those of the nearest spectators and then looked ahead to the newly erected scaffold standing just a few yards away. Waiting nearby was a dark-haired man of dishevelled appearance. With four paces to go, Masekala clenched his jaws tight. Suddenly, he stopped in mid-stride and took a step to his left until he stood face-to-face with the unkempt, dark-haired man. The unexpected movement caught his escort off-guard. Before anyone could react he spat a small stone and a large mouthful of spittle into the face of the stunned onlooker. Saliva covered the man's eyes, nose and mouth. Masekala watched as his victim's face registered first shock, then outrage.

Jango reacted furiously to the insult; he pulled his gun from its holster and without hesitation fired two quick shots into Masekala's stomach, before anyone could intervene. Instantly, the Indian crumpled and collapsed to the ground with blood gushing from the holes in his belly. A deathly hush descended on the crowd as the townsfolk waited for the next move. Women shielded their eyes from the sight of Masekala's blood staining the dusty soil; a few children ran away, others remained frozen to the spot.

With a deft flick of his wrist a Mexican gentleman standing a few paces away used his bullwhip to flick the revolver out of Jango's hand. With another movement the Mexican contrived to make the plaited leather thong curl tightly around his neck; with a sharp tug, Jango was thrown off balance and he fell to the floor, twisting and cursing. He appealed to the crowd: "Fuckin' red bastard! D'you see what that savage did to me! He was gonna die anyway!"

O'Hara was angry that the hanging detail's legitimate duty had been usurped by a hothead. He needed to restore his authority and barked a command at the marshal, ignoring all etiquette: "I want that man arrested – *now!* Throw him inside!"

The marshal and his deputies rapidly complied, as O'Hara knelt to examine the fatally wounded Masekala. The Indian looked into the major's eyes and gasped in his tribal tongue: "I said I would not hang, major. I die a warrior's death!"

As the last breath left Masekala's body O'Hara allowed the weight of the dead Indian chief to sink to the ground.

A voice behind him spoke softly. "Perhaps you should not blame the little hombre too much, señor?"

With his vaqueros flanking him on either side, the silver bearded Mexican wore his finely cut clothes with the ease of an established 'grandee'. His demeanor was that of a man who knew his own worth and was accustomed to being treated with a degree of deference.

O'Hara pointed at the dead Indian. "You understood what he said?"

"Si, señor. Our Indian friend chose to insult the hombre most likely to put a bullet in him. He provoked him on purpose. Masekala was a man full of pride. It was his way of dying with honor."

"Yeah, I guess you're right," conceded O'Hara. "Forgive me, señor, I don't know your name... ?"

"Perdone, señor. I am Don Jose, Antonio Mendoza-Castillos. I am here to purchase a new blood line of Hereford bulls for my rancho in California - for me, it is a working holiday."

O'Hara introduced himself and shook the Mexican's hand as they watched the body of Masekala being carried away.

He turned to his new acquaintance. "Won't you join me for a drink, Don Jose?"

"Muchas gracias, major – but this town is a little too crowded for my liking. Please be my guest, instead: join me at my camp and taste the wines of California! I will get my daughter, 'Bellita, to prepare a meal for you – she is a most excellent cook. I promise you won't regret it!"

6. THE LAW OF ANGER

On stormy days when fierce hurricanes blow, many kinds of plant seed get scattered over a wide area, wherever the breeze takes them. Occasionally, they find the right conditions for growth; they germinate, take root, and may even start to obliterate the indigenous species.

In similar manner, when news spread of the yellow nuggets discovered in the Black Hills of Dakota, men blew in from all over the world. For those with whom 'Lady Luck' was riding, there were great riches to be had.

Hundreds of men begged, borrowed, murdered and plundered with one thought in mind: to make enough money to claim a stake which would turn their dreams into reality. Those that succeeded flooded into the mountains, turning the air blue with their profanities as their work ended in disappointment. Prospectors dug wherever they could, with dire consequences for the countryside: rivers and streams became polluted; animals large and small were killed for food until there hardly seemed to be a jackrabbit or a moorhen left alive; even the prairie dogs disappeared.

There was one area of the Black Hills that all the Indian tribes regarded as sacred: they believed it to be the resting place of the supreme being, 'Manitou', the Great Spirit of the Indian nation. Groups of Indians would occasionally venture there to pay homage to 'Mother Earth', or to find solace in their grief - or just to commune with the spirits.

The Indians visiting the area were usually sufficient in number to scare off the most rapacious gold hunters.

But there was one band of men more determined than the others. They were well provisioned and knowledgeable about the terrain. They had chosen their site carefully, pitched their stake and started to dig. Within just a few days, their gamble had begun to pay off - as they struck a seam of paydirt that was rich enough to give six men a sack full of gold each, after just two months of laboring. After six months of excavation the vein had started to peter out and the digging had become tedious and backbreaking. Besides that, a couple of the men were beginning to show signs of scurvy for the want of fresh green vegetables.

When they had first discovered the gold they had

come to a mutual agreement. It was decided that four men would dig, whilst two stood watch. The shift would change every two hours, and it was agreed that at the first sign of any Indians, everyone would defend the diggings until their life was spent.

Late one afternoon Jango came scurrying into the camp: "Stash the picks and grab yer rifles – Indians!" He leapt from his saddle and quickly pulled his horse into the thick brush. "There's a couple o'scouts headed this way," he explained breathlessly, "there's gotta be a whole posse of red-skins right behind!"

The six men immediately grabbed their rifles and took up pre-planned defensive positions. Tensely, they waited for the arrival of the scouts, not daring to move or speak. After an hour of expectant waiting had passed, one of the men - an English merchant who had jumped ship the previous winter – whispered:

"Are you sure about this Jango, mate? You sure it wasn't a bleedin' illusion?"

"As sure as I'm standing here shittin' on your boots, Limey!" Flashing a quick look at his boots the ex-sailor moved a few steps away.

Jango's temper was on a short fuse and he was just about to launch himself at the sailor when Quinn, the big Irishman, stepped in between them.

"Behave yourselves now, d'you hear? You'll be the death of us all! Shut up and listen!"

The sailor broke the mood with a smile and a laugh: "Look at us quarrelling with each other like old women! We're stretched out here like six blokes waitin' for some dockside tarts to 'appen along!" He guffawed and started to walk into the clearing.

"Be quiet, you fucking idiot!" growled Quinn, his voice full of menace. Suddenly, they could all hear the stomp of unshod hooves dislodging pebbles strewn along the track. They threw themselves down into the greenery and peered out.

"It's two squaws!" Jango dug the big man next to him in the ribs. "Hey Quinn!" He shook his head in disbelief. "We've been hiding from a couple o'squaws!"

Keeping his voice low, he whispered to the cockney sailor: "Hey Limey, here come your whores!"

The unsuspecting females let their horses proceed at their own pace along a thick growth of fruit bushes.

"What d'ya say Quinn - do we have us some fun? They're all on their lonesome and the claim's finished!" Jango looked towards the others for confirmation of the backing he sensed was there. Two of the men nodded their acceptance of the plan.

"We could be away to Faber's Creek by sundown,

and by noon sun-up, enjoying the delights of civilization once again!" enthused Jango. His convivial manner changed abruptly as he ran the tip of his tongue over his dried lips. "I've always fancied me a piece of red ass... C'mon, Quinn, what d'ya say?" He spilled the words out impatiently.

Quinn was the leader of the party by virtue of his size and character. He had a no-nonsense approach to problems and was adept at diffusing squabbles amongst the others in the camp. Usually, he did little to conceal his contempt for Jango: the two were merely partners of convenience. His religious morality would not allow him to condone Jango's suggestion, but he had to walk a thin line between exercising his authority and cutting the men some slack. He had thought about breaking camp soon, in any case, as he wanted to get back to Boston; years before, he had promised his family he would open a bar there, if he ever had the cash to build one…

He put it to the others to decide.

"I'm with Jango," said the first, cuffing his nose against the sleeve of his dirty, red-checkered shirt.

"You would be!"

"Me too, Quinn. I'm with Jango!" The young fresh-faced cowboy looked at the space between Quinn's boots.

"Billy!" Quinn's voice conveyed his surprise and

disapproval.

Billy whispered his reply defiantly: "I've seen men lift the hair of Injuns, just for a two dollar bounty - I don't wanna kill'em, for Chrissake!"

"And you?" said Quinn, pointing at the cockney sailor.

"Well, it's like this Quinn. As I see it, women's bodies were made by nature to do just one thing. They need a bit of male company just like we need them - and as they're Indians we don't need to be too polite about it. It's bin a long time 'an I'm feeling very 'orny." He smiled at Quinn and clenched his fist in a gesture of bonhomie. "C'mon!" he urged. "Let's do 'em!"

Quinn came from a strict Catholic background and he found such talk offensive. He reacted instinctively:

"Shut your mouth!"

The cockney sailor realized he had hit the wrong note and fell silent.

Quinn turned to the one man he respected. "And what about you Chuck?"

Chuck was a family man of a somewhat sensitive character. He was better educated than the others and often expressed concern for the welfare of people he knew – and, indeed, the horses the party depended on. He was out of his element amongst the hardened souls of the western frontier and was uncomfortable with the situation he now found himself in.

He looked at Quinn and blinked several times before he spoke: "Well, I - I don't think we should..." He hesitated. "Maybe we..." The burden of speaking against the proposal overwhelmed him and he heaved his shoulders up with a deep intake of breath before looking down at the ground. "Well, I suppose... they're only Indian women, after all."

"It's five to one against ya, Quinn!" sniggered Jango triumphantly.

Unaware of the discussion concerning them the two young women lingered at the same spot for a while as they busily gathered the ripening fruit.

Quinn could not contain his anger any longer. He looked up at the sky and raised his arms in supplication. "Would all the saints protect me!" he intoned. He looked around at the others, but his words were addressed to a deity: "Mother of God protect me from these stupid bastards!"

Shaking his head, but still in control of his emotions, when he spoke again his voice was low and scornful. He made no attempt to hide his disdain: "Look at you! I never saw a sorrier looking bunch! You're all thinking with your pricks instead of your brains! Have you taken a good look at those squaws? Well, it's obvious even at this distance that they're Sasquatchoni. You obviously won't heed my counsel, but my advice to you all is - forget it!"

Quinn flicked his hands up as though discarding a soiled rag and walked off towards the horses. "Fuck the lot of yer! You can burn in Hell for all I care!"

"Where you going, Quinn?" enquired the anxious Chuck.

Quinn shot a glance over his shoulder: "Suddenly this place stinks - and so does the company!"

Despite his disapproval of their intentions the others knew that Quinn would make no move to warn the young women of what was to occur. He always obeyed the Westerner's rule of self-preservation, which had served him so well up this point: *Look to yourself*.

They watched as he threw a saddle onto his horse and began to pack his gear.

Jango was taking a keener look at the unsuspecting squaws. He gripped the British sailor's arm tightly as he stared. With a detached excitement he muttered: "By Quinn's Holy Ghost, I do believe he's right! They *are* Sasquatchoni! I've seen that big'un before!"

Unconsciously, Jango touched his permanently

swollen ear. "We're gonna have us a good time, Limey!"

The squaws were young and did not know that they were breaking one of the strictest rules of their tribe. It had been ordained by the Sasquatchoni tribal elders that women should travel in groups when gathering food in the Black Hills and that warriors should always accompany them. By taking such precautions they could avoid molestation by the white man. But the women had no warriors with them…

They got off their horses and began to pick the blueberries. Slowly, they made their way along the bushes, laughing and talking, stopping occasionally to eat the biggest fruit and throwing the rest into their baskets. Preoccupied with their task, they failed to notice the twitching ears of their mustangs as they moved unhurriedly from bush to bush. The horses were restless, aware that hidden eyes were watching them…

The bushes came alive as the patience of the excited men snapped and they were unable to restrain themselves any longer. They burst forth to catch the women, shouting and swearing amongst themselves. The mustangs were nervous and jumpy, ready to run.

"Grab those damn ponies will yuh, yuh stupid

whoresons - get' em under cover!" screamed Jango. His command was obeyed and in seconds all was silent. The women were restrained, gagged and dragged off into the trees. When they were concealed from view, the prospectors felt safe.

The mocking voice of Jango called out: "Hey Quinn, come on over here an' see what I got!"

The big man ignored the voice and carried on gathering his goods.

"Whoa - steady girl!" said Jango as he clasped the statuesque Chioe. The men held her arms tightly behind her back as the sailor yanked her friend's long dark hair. Zia yelped in pain as her head was pulled sharply downwards.

Jango glared at Chioe and rasped: "Yuh don't remember me, do yuh sweetheart? But I remember yuh – sure I do!" He nodded his head in heated anticipation. "Yessireebob! I couldn't forget a body like that!"

Chioe's eyes flared as she recognized the man's dishevelled appearance, his leering grin and his strong body odor.

"Yeah, that's it! You remember me now, don't yuh? Ha, sure yuh do!" A cynical smile spread unevenly across his face, taunting her. "Old Jedediah Jones trading post! I took a whupping over yuh that day. I fancied yuh then, an'

I fancy yuh now!"

Relaxing his grip, Jango let his fingers slowly caress the curve of her neck. He drew his hand down by degrees until it fully cupped her left breast. Their eyes locked as they stared hard at each other. He fondled the firm contours of her bosom with deliberation, lustfully running his hand over her rounded hips and thighs, then gradually down over the bulge of her stomach until it rested just above her crotch. Then he broke the spell.

"Yeah, I'm sure gonna enjoy this!"

As the first wave of petrifying fear left her, Chioe knew she had to react quickly. The intentions of the white men were all too obvious and she knew instinctively that if she did not try to escape at this moment she would have little choice but to submit to their assault. Struggling vigorously, she jabbed her upraised knee into the testicles of the man holding her right arm. As he gasped in sudden agony he briefly released her arm and she was able to reach for her small skinning knife. In a swift movement she slashed at Jango's body, her blade cutting into the fleshy part of his shoulder. Jango punched her in defense before he had registered any pain, his bone hard fist clubbing against the side of her head.

Quinn turned just in time to see Jango striking Chioe. Stunned by the weight of the punch, she fell to the ground heavily. As she tried to rise to her feet, Jango began kicking her.

Quinn did not want to be party to a rape. He had therefore decided to take his share of the goods and quit the camp - but he was still seething with anger at the actions of his companions. He pulled his horse to a halt and looked back again. He saw Jango kick the squaw in the stomach. As she cried out in pain a thunderous mood descended on the Irishman. "That stinking little bastard!" he muttered.

He dismounted and ran back to confront Jango. Glaring at him he shouted: "I'll not see the poor thing mistreated by the likes o 'you," and then slammed a right-handed punch into Jango's belly. As Jango bent double Quinn's knee came up to meet his victim's chin. Blood spurted from Jango's mouth as he bit his tongue with the impact and stumbled backwards. Quinn kicked him to the ground and drew his gun. He stood over the semi-conscious man and hissed: "You vicious bastard, you... I should kill you here and now. It's been a long time coming you piss-taking little runt!"

He looked at the others, his blood boiling with rage: "And as for you four miserable excuses - you call yourselves men? You're animals, d'you hear? Animals! I should gut shoot every damn one o'you!"

The others said nothing, knowing the enraged Quinn was quite capable of carrying out his murderous threat. They eyed him warily, each man conscious that one word out of place could provoke a deadly response from the Irishman.

Chioe's vision was blurred and she groaned as her cheekbone blackened and swelled. Quinn kneeled down to examine her injury. He looked at Chuck and said: "Get me some water and be quick about it. We may still get out of this alive, I'll…"

The blow upon his back was so violent that Quinn went sprawling alongside the unconscious girl. Though dazed, he pushed himself upright as dark red blood began to seep between his teeth. His face contorted with the effort and he felt suddenly weak. He looked down to see a blood-soaked pickaxe point protruding from his chest. As blood frothed beneath his shirt his lungs wheezed their last few breaths and the big man's eyes rolled in their sockets. His mouth silently formed two more words: "God help…" Then he collapsed, face down in the dirt.

"That's the last time that Irish bastard tells me what t'do!" said Jango, as he wiped the blood away from his face with his shirt. He screamed at the corpse: "Say 'hello' to St Patrick on your way up to those pearly gates, Quinn - and spit in his eye for me!" He began to laugh, nervously. The others stared blankly at him, unsure what to say or do. Jango continued: "He had no call t'do that! We don't fight our own out here!"

Jango sensed that he had not yet won the others over, so he decided to appeal to their baser instincts. "Now we get to enjoy the women - *and* share Quinn's gold! How 'bout that!" he said.

No one moved and not one word was spoken.

"C'mon!" urged Jango. He spat more bloodstained spittle at Quinn's body, then gritted his teeth and gave the men an uncompromising look. "C'MON!" he urged.

His co-conspirators were hard-bitten men who had experienced the rigors of the trail, and all of them were familiar with death. Nevertheless, they stood mesmerized by the horror of the scene they had just witnessed and it took them some time to recover. Their minds were rattled at the loss of Quinn and they were all shocked by the violence of his end.

But the big man was gone and there was now no brake on their thoughts and deeds. Jango was right: they were now richer than ever, and there was no scowling Irishman to disapprove of their decisions. They were inflamed by greed and their imaginations were brimming with pent-up sexual desire. The gun was ready and loaded; it needed one word to pull the trigger.

At that precise moment, Zia chose to make a break for freedom. Jango yelled furiously at Chuck: "Yuh stupid sonofabitch, grab her!"

The men fell upon the hapless women like a pack of wolves.

"Hey!" warned the cockney sailor striking out viciously at Billy, "wait a minute, old son. Don't you know the rules? 'Age before Beauty.' You wait till I've had my turn!"

Casting aside their inhibitions the diggers fought rabidly with each other for the discreditable privilege of being the first to ravish the women.

With their eyes wide open, Chioe and Zia stared silently back at the prospectors in abject fear for their lives. In a few moments the girls' screams could be heard through the trees as the men sated their lust, savagely and completely...

Unknown to the prospectors, two young Sasquatchoni boys had been stalking Chioe and Zia from the moment they had vacated their lodge. The youngsters were deeply immersed in a game of 'warriors'. They had fashioned small bows and arrows from sticks and were practicing the art of tracking people. In their minds they were Indian heroes from ages past – resolute, fearless and wise. They had decided that their challenge would be to track the women as far as they could, without being discovered by them. In this endeavor they had been very successful - right up to the point where the men had abducted the squaws. The boys had watched from a distance as the women were taken and they were shocked by the violence of the white men. They knew immediately that the situation was serious; suddenly, the game was a game no more: they had a real challenge to rise to. After a hurried discussion they decided to run back to the Sasquatchoni camp to tell the warriors of the tribe what had occurred... the men would know what to do.

The boys started backtracking as quickly as they could, making full use of every available piece of cover. They took care not to startle any birds or other animals, fearing that the white men might investigate the cause of a sudden noise. Their stealthy retreat around the hill took longer than they had anticipated, and it was some time before they were beyond rifle range. When they were a safe distance away, they ran at full pelt, heedless of their own safety, aware that the women's lives might depend upon their speed. Despite their headlong plunge through the forest they could only travel as fast as their legs would carry them, and they still had to run four miles back to the lodge of Chief Tonala to raise the alarm.

When the boys finally arrived at the Sasquatchoni encampment they breathlessly informed the tribal elders about the plight of Chioe and Zia. Chief Tonala was enraged and full of fatherly concern for his daughter and her best friend. He ordered RoShann and his friend Pancifico to take a small group of their bravest men to rescue the women. They grabbed their weapons and set out on horseback.

After riding at breakneck speed through the clearings and along narrow trails to an uninhabited region of the hills, the warriors finally arrived at the prospector's diggings. The white men had evidently broken camp and departed. In their drunken state they had neglected to tidy-up the area – and it was not just the smouldering fire that betrayed their recent presence.

Unaware of the two boys, they had expended their carnal desires on the women without compunction. The squaws had resisted fiercely at first, until they were clubbed and stabbed into submission. Scraps of their torn clothing and bloodspots on the ground provided ample evidence of their rape and battery. When the men had drunk too much whiskey to continue, they had dragged the girls' lifeless bodies back to their pitch and thrown them into the excavations. Then, they had hastily covered up the bodies with brushwood.

After only a brief search of the area RoShann and his men quickly found the women's bodies: they were bloodied, naked and stiffening with rigor mortis. The degradation they had suffered before dying made the warriors angry – they demanded vengeance.

RoShann reached down to cover the bare figures of his sister, Chioe, and her friend, Zia. Their throats had been cut and their bodies mutilated. He choked back a cry of anguish. With dark emotions twisting his face he ordered a travois to be constructed so that the bodies could be carried back to Chief Tonala.

"Let us ride after the white men, RoShann!" urged the warriors. "They cannot be far away. We can still catch them!"

"No, you forget! Pancifico and his warriors have ridden ahead by another route to intercept them. Between us, we will box them in. We have already pushed our horses hard – they must rest. That is my word."

In the waning light of early evening, Pancifico's scouts appeared at the prospector's camp carrying torches. They rode straight toward Roshann and his men, who were waiting impatiently for news.

As he approached, the warrior pointed towards the trail. "We have found tracks; five men with pack horses!"

RoShann instantly surmised the intentions of the prospectors: "They are heading for Fort Kearny," he said, mounting his horse. In a grimly determined voice he vowed: "We will find them. They must not reach the fort!"

* * * *

"RoShann!"

There was no reply so Pancifico tried again, until something stirred in the gathering night.

"Pancifico," answered RoShann softly. "You have found them?"

"Yes, over there!" Pancifico's sturdy, familiar figure gestured in the direction of a cluster of trees. RoShann reminded himself of his father's order: *'They must be taken alive.'*

He whistled a signal to indicate that all of the Sasquatchoni warriors should dismount. In a few moments, he had issued his orders and the warriors dispersed, their eyes by now accustomed to the darkness.

The hushed silence of the night lay over the earth like a blanket; the occasional snuffle of an unseen, nocturnal prowler was the only distraction. The prospectors were lying like fallen logs, exhausted by their long day and their uncomfortable ride. They were all sleeping, deeply and contentedly - except for Chuck, who was keeping watch.

Chuck Williams was by nature a gentle man, quite uninclined to violence of any sort. As he ruminated on what had happened to the Indian women, he was filled with remorse. Though he had not taken part in their murder, the large amount of alcohol he had consumed had finally allowed him to participate in their rape. But the effect had worn off and he now felt ashamed at his actions. As he pulled the blanket tighter around his shoulders he stared dully at the embers of the small fire. Someone had to stand guard at night – and, as he could not sleep, he had gladly volunteered.

He looked at his slumbering associates and noted how innocent they all appeared to be. They were arrayed like children, curled up in different postures with their limbs sprawled out at odd angles.

A miserable thought passed through his head: *'Innocent? God knows they're not that! Why did I let that mad bastard Jango talk me into it? Why? I should have tried to stop him... but I didn't. He killed them, and that was just plain wrong... wrong! There was no need to use a knife on them!'*

He spread his hands in despair. *'I should have backed Quinn... Hell! It was that damn gold; it clouded my judgement, stole my senses. It's cursed!'*

Chuck replayed the events of the last twelve hours over in his mind. But nothing helped; he knew he was simply making excuses to justify his own shortcomings. He could not reconcile his actions with his conscience. The echo of Jango's phrase, *'they're only Indian women!'* returned to taunt him again and again. He stared into the fire as the flames danced amongst the shadows, conjuring up nightmare visions of the recent past.

At last, dispirited and weary, he covered his face. He dug his fingers into his skin trying to blot out his eyes. The hypnotic glow and warmth of the fire made him feel drowsy and he awoke with a jerk. His thoughts whirled as he fought to reassure himself.

'What was that? Did something move just then? An Indian in the shadows!

Nah! Just get a grip, boy, you're a fool! God dammit! I'm so tired… No one saw us, and nobody knows we're here. The bodies are covered up and it'll be days before they're found - if ever… …I'll be glad when we reach Fort Kearny, that's for sure! I'm getting the willies…'

Some distance away a wolf raised its head to emit a melancholy howl; the horses moved about skittishly as a slight breeze blew up. It was too much for Chuck. He took fright; he needed to move… Something wasn't right and he had to tell the others. Spooked by the messages his brain was receiving Chuck threw off his blanket intending to rouse them, but a glancing blow to his head made him wince and fall back. Strong hands stifled his warning shout before his lips could move.

Working silently, RoShann and the other warriors seized each of the white men in turn. They were gagged and bound and tied onto their horses; then all trace of their presence at the campsite was thoroughly erased.

The rising sun slowly pushed back the darkness. Strong rays of crimson sunlight broke through a dark blue sky, bringing color and life to the harsh landscape. The only noise to disturb the morning's tranquility was the muffled sound of hoof beats and the creaking of leather saddles as RoShann led his captives to where Chief Tonala was waiting with a large gathering of the Sasquatchoni tribe.

As the troupe entered the grassy glade the five white men became aware of their perilous situation. The tall Sasquatchoni onlookers pushed and shoved each other in their angry attempts to confront the prospectors. People at the front of the throng struck out at the men with anything that came to hand.

At a signal from RoShann the procession came to a

halt and the prisoners were pulled from their horses. They stood awkwardly with their hands and feet still bound. As Tonala rode up to them they grouped together nervously. The chief held his lance aloft to signal silence from the crowd. Then he addressed the prisoners directly:

"I am Tonala, Chief of the Sasquatchoni! Look long, and take in everything you see…" He waved his arm around in a semi-circle. "This is where your lives will end!"

RoShann translated the chilling words into English for the benefit of the prisoners. As the meaning sank into their minds they looked bewildered. None of them had seriously considered that the Indians would have the temerity to execute them. Not here… not with Fort Kearny so close. They looked at the tall, majestic figure of Tonala, his feathered cloak ruffling in the early morning breeze.

The chief spoke again: "When the white man digs for gold, he is as sly as the kit fox; when he kills, he is as ruthless as the wolf. But unlike the wolf, he does not kill just for food. He also kills for pleasure – as you killed our women! Therefore, I say - your lives will be forfeited so that our daughters' spirits may rest!" Tonala's finger pointed at each individual standing in front of him, slowly moving around the group, accusing and indicting them.

The miner in the red-checkered shirt was trembling

visibly. He blurted out: "No! You can't do that! I have a wife and young children waiting for me. Please, I beg you," - he fell to his knees shaking his head, "you can't do that!" He began to sob like a child.

The other prospectors chimed in, each man proclaiming his innocence.

"'Hey, just a minute, chief!" protested the cockney sailor. "I'm a British subject - I shouldn't even be here! I only joined up with this lot to look for gold, nuffin' else! 'Ere, tell you what – we found some, too! Show 'im the gold someone, where's it gone? We found gold - quite a bit. It was in the saddlebags. I'd like you to know how sorry I am about what happened to these women – which I had nuffin' to do wiv, by the way - and as a means of showing how sad I feel, I would like to donate everything we found to the chief. There's more, too - some extra, which I buried!"

Jango interjected: "Hey, what are you sayin', you got more than us? You cheatin' Limey bastard!"

The Englishman ignored him and continued to smile desperately at Tonala as a bead of sweat trickled down his forehead. "I'll tell you where it is, chief, if you'll just accept this gift from me and allow me to walk away. Err… with my condolences, of course. As for the others here, well… you can do what you like wiv 'em. Another thing to bear in mind is that if you finish me off, you'll be at war with Great Britain! There's no need for that, chief. Take the gold and my regrets and let's part on decent terms, eh?"

When he heard the translation Tonala threw his lance forcefully into the ground. The miners' guilt was already firmly established but he had wanted to hear their explanations for the killings.

"Enough! We need no gold – that is white man's wampum. There is no amount that could save your life! Why did you kill our young women?" he demanded. "Why? You used their bodies then stole their lives!"

Looking uneasily at each other, none of the prospectors spoke.

"White men never understand," continued Tonala. "You take much from the Indian," - he spat the words out bitterly, "and give nothing in return. You take our land, you take our animals, and you enslave our women and children. Now you kill our young women for pleasure!"

The people acknowledged his words noisily. All eyes were upon the prospectors - who, in turn, were staring at Tonala.

Jango pushed his way forwards. "Yuh have the wrong man here, Tonala," he protested, "I'm innocent! Hell, we all are!"

As RoShann translated his words Tonala reacted with

fury. His powerful arms grabbed hold of Jango, lifted him up and shook him around like a woman shakes a buffalo robe. Jango could feel his senses blacking out; his neck was on the verge of breaking as his shirtfront tore apart. The chief dropped him suddenly and he collapsed in a heap.

"White scum! You had no reason to kill them!" Tonala threw away the torn pieces of shirt still in his hands. Jango protested again from the ground: "It wasn't us, believe me! It must've bin some other miners an' that's the truth! There's lots round here!"

"Your face is a liar's face! Make your mark!" said the chief.

A puzzled Jango carefully sketched his initial in the dust. Tonala looked coldly at the letter 'J' drawn in the soil. Then he lifted his lance to indicate that a pathway should open up in the crowd to allow others to pass through. A small group of warriors approached. They were carrying three stretchers, two of which they lowered gently to the ground and placed side by side; the third was laid in front of the white men. Female attendants rolled back the robes to expose the bodies.

Tonala turned to the corpse lying in front of the prisoners and pointed at the pickaxe embedded in Quinn's chest. Burned into the axe handle was a large letter 'J'.

"It was them!" Jango groveled on his hands and

knees before the Indian chief. "They made me do it, I swear! I tried to hold them back, but they wouldn't listen to me! They had it in their heads to have those women - I'm just caught up in all this! Lemme go, please! I won't say a word to anyone about what happened here. I'll leave the territory, you'll never see me again!"

This was more than the English sailor could stomach. He lunged at Jango, hissing: "I'll cut your bleedin' tongue out for that, you lying bastard! So help me I will!"

Tonala's warriors struggled to restrain the enraged Englishman but were too slow to stop Chuck moving forward. "Stop it!" he screamed at Jango. "Stop your whimpering you goddam sonofabitch!" He placed the sole of his boot on Jango's shoulder and pushed him over with a contemptuous kick. "It's finished! We're all gonna die because of you! You killed those women and now you're tryin' to bargain your way out. You're one hell of a piece of work, Jango! A gutless, soulless, murdering shithead! You disgust me! Whatever happens now, you've got it coming. So have we all!" He looked at the others with an accusatory eye. "Speaking for my own part, well... I'm gonna go with whatever dignity I can pull together; that's all that's left for me to do!"

Tonala stood beside Chioe's corpse. With a sorrowful face he addressed the prisoners: "This is the body of my daughter! Her blood was my blood, her flesh my flesh."

RoShann translated the words for the conspirators as Tonala waited. "No more will she greet me, as the birds greet the dawn. No more will her love enrich me."

Chuck stuttered: "Yes, I understand. We're all to blame for their deaths; why, some of us just by being there and doing nothing. I'm sorry!"

Tonala glanced at Chuck. He perceived that the white man who had spoken was no warrior; yet he was the only one of the captives with sufficient courage to openly confess to his misdeeds. Experience had taught Tonala that the weak could find strength in the face of death, and so it appeared to be with this man. As their eyes met there was an instant of melding: in a moment each knew the other's mind and understood the finality of what had occurred and the inevitability of what would follow. Explanations, conciliatory gestures and apologies were conveyed in a sad and silent appraisal of each other.

The weeping parents of Zia, supported by other family members and friends found their way to the front of the gathering.

"The white men must die, Tonala! They must know pain as my child knew pain! My child must be avenged!" Zia's mother prostrated herself before Tonala, beseeching his acquiescence.

Tonala nodded at one of his most trusted men. A command was given and each prospector in turn was forcibly stripped naked before being tied between two upright posts. Some of the prospectors still protested their innocence.

"God damn your soul, Tonala!" Jango cursed vehemently. "May yuh rot in Hell, yuh red-skinned bastard! We got a right to be tried by a US judge and jury! It's a white man's law that rules now!"

When RoShann translated Jango's last-ditch gambit Tonala dismissed it, replying succinctly: "The strong dictate the law, and today our anger makes us strong. Our daughters' spirits call for vengeance and they will be satisfied."

Young Billy let out a plaintive cry: "Please God, save us! I don't want to die! Please save us, Lord!"

The men writhed as their arms and legs were tied to the posts with leather strips. When the task was done Tonala stood in front of them. In a firm voice he declared:

"Your missionaries speak of your God; they say he died for me. That was unnecessary, for he caused me no wrong. You, however – you have torn my heart from my body. Now it is time for you to honour your God." He paused, then continued: "You will all die for me!"

The prospectors struggled as large mounds of dry

twigs were placed beneath their outstretched legs. When all was ready, a gesture from Tonala saw each of the mounds ignited with a burning brand. Slowly, the smoke twirled upward, choking the men. As they spluttered and gasped for breath, the flames caught hold and grew in size until they began to lap at the captives' thighs.

From the corner of his mouth the sailor spat at Jango: "This is all 'cause of you! They're sending us to Hell! They're gonna bleedin' *cook* us!" He screeched in agony as the flames flickered higher, searing his legs.

The mother of the dead Zia ran forward and slashed at Jango's groin. His piercing scream was the signal for the other tribeswomen to lacerate the genitals of the prisoners with their skinning knives.

Tonala turned and spoke to RoShann. The younger man placed a heavy arrow into the nock of his hunting bow and aimed quickly. He bent the bow to its maximum extent and fired the arrow through Chuck's head to ensure that he died before the women could reach him.

The others were left to burn until their screams subsided and their flesh turned black.

The deaths of the prospectors went some way towards assuaging the Sasquatchonis' righteous anger at the savagery of the men's deeds. But there was to be no long-term respite from the predations of other white settlers. The hungry land grabbers staked out their plots and rushed back to the land registry office at Faber's Creek to file their claims. Few questioned the morality of the arrangement: it was their right under the law, facilitated by the government in Washington and the constitution.

As more and more Europeans invaded traditional Indian hunting grounds some native tribes went on the rampage. Knowing nothing of the white man's civil law, the Indians were incapable of objecting to the continual encroachments on their land. In a bid to get the army involved, a group of town speculators set fire to the Sasquatchoni maize fields - hoping that the tribe would retaliate. But Tonala's shrewd leadership intervened and his wisdom prevailed: the loss of the corn was a severe blow for the Sasquatchoni tribe's winter survival but the provocateurs' names and faces were unknown. Tonala counseled that to react against the local white population indiscriminately would be unjust and would have undesired consequences. Instead, a delegation of chiefs was sent to see the marshal at Faber's Creek to request that the guilty men be arrested and punished in accordance with the white man's law. An investigation was held, but - as many Indians expected - none of the twenty or so men involved were charged.

Tonala was not surprised when RoShann reported that the businessmen of Faber's Creek were refusing to supply the Sasquatchoni people with grain. He said simply: "If one lodge is closed to us, we will try another. We will make sacrifices to the Great Spirit, and all will be well."

7. SEEDS OF DESTRUCTION

With his elbows resting on the desktop Colonel Austin rubbed his hands through his thinning hair and released a deep sigh. His campaign against the Indian tribes had not gone according to plan. The troopers were chasing and engaging Sioux and Cheyenne warriors, but on many occasions they came off second best; the dead and wounded were proof of that. The dispatches he had received from Washington were not comfortable reading for him; some were openly critical of his command.

A knock on the door interrupted his thoughts. When he looked up, the tall figure of O'Hara stood before him.

"Yes major, what is it?"

The blue eyes looking back at him blinked. Colonel Austin returned the stare with restrained animosity.

O'Hara spoke firmly: "There's a deputation of Sasquatchoni chiefs outside. They say they want to speak with you urgently. It's an opportunity I thought you shouldn't miss, colonel."

Blowing down his nose in exasperation, the colonel slammed his hand down on the desk and stood up. "Once more, major, I don't need you to remind me of my duties. You are aware of my orders on this subject. Are you deliberately trying to provoke me?"

"No, sir."

"Then you know that no Indians are to be allowed into the fort. I don't trust them and I've no intention of endlessly negotiating with them. Their response to my reasonable demands has been negative." Breathing deeply Austin moved away from his desk, and then returned to take his seat. "Therefore, major, until Tonala makes a final decision and moves his people into a reservation, I refuse to see him or his emissaries."

O'Hara leaned forward to look directly at Austin, his knuckles resting on the desk.

"D'you know why they won't move, colonel? The ground in the reservations is stony and bare, and there's no wood! How're they going to cook their meat - or keep warm? How're they going build a lodge?" He paused to glance at the prairie visible through the window. "Why should they move when these lands are their traditional hunting grounds?"

"I'm afraid I can't debate the matter with you, major," objected the colonel. "My job - and yours – is to act on requests we receive from The Commissioner for Indian Affairs."

"That's all they are, colonel - requests!"

"Damn you, O'Hara, our representatives know what they're doing!" snapped the colonel.

"Do they?" growled O'Hara. With a pointed look at the colonel he saluted and walked out of the room.

The negro sentry saluted as O'Hara approached him. "Open the gate, trooper!" said the major curtly.

"But, sir! The colonel's order?"

"D'you want your ass kicked?" enquired O'Hara fiercely.

The sentry shook his head. "Well lookin' at the size o'your feet major, I think you might need 'em both to kick this ass!" He laughed and slapped the big yams of his backside. Both men smiled as the fort entrance gates were swung wide open.

Outside, the Indian delegation was waiting with patient expectation. They were accustomed to waiting: they waited for the buffalo to return, and for the maize in the fields to grow. Each day, they prayed for the sun to rise again, and for the cooling winds to blow. Stolidly, they had waited for the major to reappear.

He moved across to speak with them.

"I'm sorry RoShann, I'm afraid the colonel cannot see you now; he has urgent military matters to attend to. He sends his respects and apologies."

RoShann was standing beside his horse. He nodded his head in comprehension at the rebuff.

"Indian chiefs always send high-ranking messengers when they do not wish to lose face. There are unspoken words in your message, O'Hara."

"I think we both appreciate the way things are, RoShann." O'Hara felt awkward and tried to soften the Indians' disappointment.

"If there's anything I can do to help you and your tribe, just ask."

RoShann meditated for a moment then came to a decision.

"Tonala sent me here to see if I could trade horses for corn. The town traders say they have none. If we do not replenish our store, we will go hungry during the winter."

"What about the reservation?" O'Hara prompted.

"My father says the tribe will not move there."

"How will you pay for corn?" asked O'Hara.

"We have gold - bags of gold, major."

O'Hara was surprised at the statement but thought it prudent not to enquire how the tribe had obtained such treasure.

"RoShann, I would like to help you but it will require that you place trust in me. Will you accept my word as an officer of the United States Army, that I will do my best to obtain food for your tribe?"

For a moment the tall young warrior stared at the timbered stockade. "No truce has been broken major, we are not at war. I have no reason not to respect your offer." He gazed at O'Hara.

"My father told me to look into the eyes of a man in order to see the true reflection of his soul. I have seen your soul. I would trust you with my life!"

Although he was an experienced and battle-hardened soldier, O'Hara could not help but be touched by RoShann's words. He outlined his plan.

"In the morning, I leave for Fort Phillips to deliver some survey plans for the Land Registry Office. While I'm there, I'll purchase three wagons and have them filled with corn. But, I'll need some help."

RoShann pointed at one of his companions.

"Mayat will meet you with warriors and the gold."

Mounting his horse he dipped his lance to salute

O'Hara, then rode away with his retinue.

* * * *

The warrior scouting ahead waved his arm to attract the party's attention. Kicking their horses, the others raced quickly over to his position. As they arrived, the scout gestured silently downward into the canyon. Far below, RoShann could see a wagon lying on its side. Scattered around it were the bodies of dead men.

A sense of foreboding fell upon him. The Sasquatchoni claimed this land belonged to them. He was curious as to who had carried out the slaughter - and why. It was an affront to the Sasquatchoni tribe – and, perhaps, a challenge to their authority. The area had to be examined for clues. Posting a lookout, he led the way downward. The paths were treacherous and it took the warriors a long time to coax their horses down the rock face. It was midday by the time they had reached ground level.

The identity of the dead men was obvious. "An army patrol," said Mayat. "No horses."

"And no rifles," added RoShann. He walked around the area to study the ground and the nearby brush. He examined the blackened stubs of the burned wooden wagon frame. The draft through the canyon had blown much of the ash away. He knelt to inspect the scorched and swollen bodies of the dead troopers. Some of them bore mutilation marks caused by vultures or other wild creatures. From such evidence he inferred that the patrolmen had been attacked and killed two or three days ago.

'Who has carried out this attack?'

Emerging from the brush, Mayat interrupted his deliberations. He was clutching two arrows.

"RoShann – look at these!" he urged.

RoShann scrutinized the arrows closely. By their markings and the colors of their flight feathers he could tell the Sioux people had made them. Another scout reported that he had found horse droppings nearby. "Many riders!"

Suddenly, a warrior appeared from beneath the torn canvas covering of a wagon that had carried a Hotchkiss machine gun. He held the weapon close to him, struggling with its weight.

"What is this!" exclaimed RoShann, startled at the discovery.

He remembered seeing a demonstration of the firepower of a Hotchkiss gun at Fort Kearny. Colonel Austin had called a meeting of the Indian chiefs to witness one in operation. The weapon was fired into a wall of sandbags. When the wall had collapsed, the tribal chiefs gave meaningful looks to each other; it was obvious that that the gun was being used to intimidate them. And it had been effective; the mere threat of its deployment was enough to cause an Indian to think hard before confronting the white men.

Such a prize had to be recovered: poles were cut and placed horizontally between two horses; then a frame was rapidly constructed to support a platform, onto which the machine gun was laid - along with its belts of ammunition and some barrels of gunpowder.

RoShann watched the warriors obliterate their tracks as they prepared to leave. He mounted his horse and led the group out of the canyon, the last two warriors dragging bushes behind them to obscure any hoof prints.

Always an early riser, the major washed and shaved, then breakfasted on hot coffee and sourdough bread. He wanted to be on the trail before sunrise. He liked to be awake before dawn; in the silent tranquillity everything seemed fresh and revitalized.

He felt the coolness of the morning and noticed that the color of the landscape was continuously changing. Already, a bright orange glow was breaking up the distant horizon. Soon, the sun would climb higher until it burned so intensely that every creature alive would scurry for the shade.

Stopping for a few moments, he watched a lone coyote scavenging around the bones of a horse. The craggy bluffs ahead dropped down and gave way to open prairie. O'Hara rode on alone. As he passed a species of cactus he took note of its small yellow flowers and shook his head in admiration at nature's miracles. He knew that within a couple of hours the sun would be so hot that rivulets of sweat would start running down his back.

As he rode, he mused on the plight of the Indian tribes. It wasn't hard to understand why they were so inflexible. They were part and parcel of nature itself, in all its grandeur - and they worked within it, in a way that white men no longer seemed willing, or able, to do. He wondered what the future might hold for them. *'Put an Indian on a reservation and you sentence him to death, more or less,'* he decided, at length. Giving his horse a pat of encouragement, he said aloud: "It's sure as hell an awkward situation."

O'Hara tried hard to recall his early childhood. He could just about remember leaving Ireland with his parents. At that time, the nation had been in the grip of the potato famine and people were desperately hungry. His mother and father had sold everything they owned to pay for their berth on the ship that took the family to America. From that moment, their lives had changed forever.

His horse danced along sideways in a frisky mood. "Whoa, boy!" he murmured.

He remembered his parents working hard to establish themselves in New York. Since that time, more and more Europeans had emigrated to the American 'Promised Land', to enjoy the freedoms its constitution proclaimed. The settlers were sold land that was already occupied; occupied by the Indians. The system had caused as much suffering as it alleviated. O'Hara had seen the problems encountered by new immigrants – unprepared, as they were, for the trials of a harsh, new life.

He thumped his thigh. "Dammit! If only they'd listen to me!" He had spoken to Tonala and the chiefs of the Sasquatchoni tribe about the need to legally protect their ownership of their ancestral territory. He had offered to stake out their land and register a claim in Tonala's name in order to obtain the deeds. But Tonala had argued against the plan: there were certain taboos and proprieties to be observed. He had insisted that no individual member of the tribe could own 'Mother Earth'. The land belonged to all Sasquatchoni for as long as they lived – just as their fathers had owned it before them. And in any case, he said, to make one's mark on a piece of paper was a custom of the white man's law, not the Indian's.

RoShann, and some of the younger chiefs who had attended missionary schools could see the logic of O'Hara's suggestion and the many good reasons why they should debate the subject again. O'Hara's thoughts swirled around the subject: it was hard to help people who wouldn't help themselves. While he brooded on the matter part of his mind remained alert, watching the trail ahead. Long experience had made it impossible for him to ever completely relax whilst riding alone. Suddenly, he became aware of a slight movement in the brush ahead of him. He looked again. It appeared to be a good place from which to launch an ambush…

Warily, he pulled his rifle from his pack, just as the giant Sasquatchonis broke cover. Mayat, the sub-chief dipped his lance in recognition and waited with his warriors for O'Hara to draw near.

After a brief exchange of greetings they rode on together to Fort Williams to purchase some corn.

* * * *

Fort Kearny was seething with a quiet, sustained anger; the air itself seemed to be alive with recriminations and curses. The troopers were angry at what had been done to their fellows. Colonel Austin was well aware of the risk he was taking with his career. *'Add yeast to a barrel of beer and the fermentation begins...'* he thought wryly.

After a few formalities had been completed he faced the assembled ranks of his soldiers and began to speak:

"Now men – listen carefully. As you know, our missing patrolmen have returned. They were found by a troop that was sent out to search for them. Sadly, each and every one of them is dead." He pointed down at the bodies lying side by side on the parade ground. "Those red skinned bastards weren't content to just kill our comrades, oh no; it seems from the evidence before our eyes, that they also took pleasure in mutilating their bodies!" He paused to let the full horror of his words sink in.

He held some arrows retrieved from the scene above his head, and continued: "These have been identified as Sioux arrows – but we are not deceived. Their use is the ploy of a cunning and ruthless enemy. I am sure that even the youngest recruit here knows that we are too far south for the Sioux nation to have been involved in such an attack."

Colonel Austin was a gifted orator with an expressive voice and he could sense that the men were with him, hanging on his every word. He continued to build his case:

"Men, the only tribe in this territory big enough and foolhardy enough to launch an attack on a well-armed column of troopers is the Sasquatchoni!" As he spoke he smashed his knuckled fist into the palm of his other hand to emphasize the words.

"D'you know why they've done this? This is an act of revenge for the burning of their lodge and the loss of their maize... They have fallen out with the townsfolk and now they blame the army for not protecting them: yes, they blame you!" He pointed at the troopers.

"The death of our boys is the Sasquatchonis' way of exacting retribution. Look at them!" He pointed his finger at the contorted bodies of the dead soldiers. "But I promise you men: so long as I am commander of Fort Kearny, no overgrown bunch of Indian savages is going to run this company off of U.S. territory!"

The troopers roared their approval and a rebel yell rose from the ranks at the rear. Austin knew he had stoked the fires of resentment perfectly, and his adrenalin was well and truly flowing; now, there had to be action to follow the words.

"Sergeant! Boots and saddle - at the double! All officers to report to me in fifteen minutes!"

The colonel tilted his head backwards to empty the

small glass of its contents. Moving his jaw sideways he rolled the liquid around with his tongue, gradually allowing the whiskey to seep down his throat. He welcomed the warm, burning sensation. "My god, that was good!" he gasped. Quickly, he refilled his glass.

Austin was in a prickly mood. He knew that his speech to the men and the version of events it had portrayed would not be welcomed by all of his officers. There was, in fact, no proof that the Sasquatchoni had carried out the slaughter; it was supposition. He didn't mind his underlings disapproving of his conclusions, so long as they continued to obey their orders and voiced any misgivings in private.

O'Hara would doubtless want to have his say at some point, and there might be others...

A knock on the door brought an end to his ruminations.

"Captain Stevens, sir!" The orderly ushered the officer in and closed the door.

The slightly built, fair-haired officer hesitated for a moment, then straightened his back and snapped out a salute. "Colonel Austin, sir!"

"Sit down Jack, there's no need to be so formal."

Stevens looked straight ahead at a commendation on the wall above Austin's head.

"Sir! With due respect for your position here, I must tell you I have grave concerns about what you said to the men just now. They are angry and looking for a fight with someone. They've seen what happened to the patrol and they want justice. But your speech amounted to an incitement to murder. Thanks to you, the men want blood - Sasquatchoni blood - even though there is no hard evidence that the tribe were involved. We've struggled hard to maintain military discipline here in the face of many provocations. Now our senior officer has given the men leave to do whatever they like with the local Indians. It could end in wholesale slaughter!"

"Captain Stevens: your objection is noted. If you would care to put your remarks in writing I will send them on to higher authority, with my countersignature. Now for God's sake, Jack, sit down and listen!" The colonel's manner was impatient, but his voice was full of authority.

Captain Stevens took a seat. "You understand, colonel - I have to make a stand. That was a rabble-rousing speech you gave and the men are in an ugly mood. The troopers are good, loyal soldiers and they take their lead from you. I think you should have urged restraint until the facts are known and left out all the fire and brimstone."

"Ordinarily, Jack, I would agree," said Colonel Austin. "But the object of the exercise is survival; yours and mine!"

"I don't follow, sir," said Captain Stevens, puzzled.

The colonel filled two whiskey glasses and pushed one across to the captain. "Your health!"

With his hands in his pockets, Austin peered through the window as a column of troopers marched past. He leaned out and shouted directives at the first sergeant, ordering him to line the men up again.

Turning, he looked once more at Captain Stevens. "On your last three patrols, Jack, you have lost a total of fifteen men. That doesn't look very good on your personal file, and it's also a black mark against my judgement and command; do you agree?"

In full flow again, the colonel did not wait for Stevens' to reply.

"I've been severely reprimanded by Washington twice whilst with this command. What d'you think will happen when the generals read my report about the loss of the patrol, for no gains - and a wagon-full of rifles stolen?"

Picking up the glass of whiskey he swallowed the contents in one gulp. "I'll tell you, Jack: Washington will demand a re-assignment. They'll say I'm not good enough to hold down a command on active service. I'll be posted to some backwater desk-job, way back east. And you – why, you'll stay at your present rank for the rest of your days, until some drunken cross-eyed brave puts a bullet in you."

Deep in thought, Captain Stevens had one arm resting upon the desktop. As he listened, he aimlessly moved the empty whiskey glass back and forth. "What you're really telling me colonel is that the Sasquatchoni tribe is the opportunity you've been waiting for?"

"Yes, Jack, yes! I couldn't have put it better myself; I knew you would read my intentions correctly. Opportunism and courage are what define the American people; this country of ours thrives on those very same principles!"

"Do those principles extend to walking all over people, colonel?"

Ignoring the pointed sarcasm Austin replied impassively: "Yes, captain – and, if necessary, killing them."

Colonel Austin watched the sulfur match flare; when it died a little he touched the flame to his cigar. Drawing deeply, he inspected the burning ash and slowly released the pungent tobacco smoke from his lungs. "When I was a young lieutenant, I heard a former President making a campaign speech. I was mightily impressed." Austin paused for a second to collect his thoughts, one finger touching his bottom lip. "The President said, and I quote:

'...the aboriginal natives of this great country, the red men, have no part to play in a civilized community such as ours. They can't adapt to an ordered way of life. They can't - because they don't want to!'"

He paused to tip a small quantity of whiskey into his glass, then swallowed it. "But it might surprise you to learn that I don't altogether share that opinion." He looked discontentedly at the cigar between his fingers and leaned over to stub it into the ashtray until it was shredded.

"Those words might apply to most of the tribes here, but the Sasquatchoni are different. They are organized. From our point of view, they are an unfortunate example to the others. They undermine our efforts to clean up this land." As he spoke, Austin counted off the attributes of the tribe on his fingers:

"They have a permanent village; they tend cattle; they grow crops; they use horses, and they send their children to the local missionary schools. The other tribes know that in winter, if conditions are difficult, they can usually trade with the Sasquatchoni to obtain provisions."

He checked the time with his pocket watch. "Now d'you see, Stevens? Without our overgrown Indian friends to support them, the other tribes would have no choice but to accede to our demands."

"Let me finish for you, colonel," interrupted Stevens. "You mean the others would have to head for the reservation to ask for food and clothing. And we would provide it on one condition – that they stayed there permanently."

Austin hesitated for a moment. "That's very perceptive of you, captain. Listen, Jack: I'm still fired with ambition, despite my gray hair. I desire respect, and I shall have it. Some day I hope to be promoted to General; but to achieve that I need to surround myself with people I can trust and rely on."

"What's in it for me?" asked Captain Stevens.

"From today, Major Stevens, you are to be my second in command! All I ask in return is that you put the lid on any qualms you may have about my methods. I know what I'm doing. Don't oppose me in this exercise. Support me all the way and we'll both benefit."

A look of startled surprise spread across the captain's face at the news of his promotion. His euphoria momentarily abated and the corner of his eye twitched as he asked: "But what about O'Hara?"

"It's been taken care of," Colonel Austin assured him. "I've had him posted to Fort Williams."

"Was that wise, sir?"

"It's my prerogative as commander; both appointments have already been recommended and approved."

"Will he talk?" queried the new major.

"I don't think so - he'll be keen to retain his dignity and too proud to express any disappointment about losing his place here. Perhaps now you can see why I made the fire and brimstone speech?"

"Yes, sir - I can. Actions speak louder than words!"

"Exactly, major. I want those men to have some fire in their bellies. I don't want them shitting in their pants the first time one of those big Sasquatchonis runs at them!"

A knock on the door broke up the conversation as the junior officers came in.

Colonel Austin knew that his army career would be effectively over if his planned attack against the Sasquatchoni did not succeed completely. He had therefore arranged for O'Hara to be posted elsewhere; the major would no doubt have been stiff-necked and willful in defense of the Indians, and could perhaps have persuaded the other officers to take his side - such was the power of his personality.

As he thought about the situation he chuckled at his own cleverness: *'You've flouted my authority once too often, Mister O'Hara! I should've had you court-martialled a long time ago. But I'm too smart for any of your tricks; after this, its goodbye and kiss my ass!'*

"Now gentlemen, your attention please!"

8. THE DEATH OF INNOCENCE

The column of eighty troopers wheeled due west on leaving Fort Kearny, their shadows growing smaller as the sun disappeared. Colonel Austin's strategy was to circle the Sasquatchoni encampment and attack it along its unguarded flank adjoining the Black Hills.

Major Jack Stevens ran a jaundiced eye over the untried troopers and shook his head at the idea of using such raw recruits to carry out the plan.

A morose thought lingered in his mind: *'I should've stood my ground and held out against this. But it's too late now.'* His doubts were followed by a cold shiver that ran down the length of his spine, reminding him of an old saying his mother had often repeated: *'Somebody just walked over your grave!'*

Full of uncertainties, Stevens muttered to himself: "Superstitious rubbish… But I wonder what price I'll truly have to pay for these?" He glanced at the rank tabs of his recent promotion – the reward for his co-operation. Responding to the pressure of his knees the horse broke into a canter and skittered away.

Colonel Austin had decided to split his command. Major Stevens was to attack from the east of the village, whilst he led the main assault from the west. The troopers were again reminded to discard anything that might jangle or reflect light.

"Remember men: we ride through the Indian encampment fast shootin' at everything and anything that moves - an' I do mean *anything!* Set fire to the lodges… When they start burning and the bugler sounds the recall, get out and retreat to the south-side of the village. Once there, you will continue to fire at will until the order is countermanded."

* * * *

Tonala was in a reflective mood. He was contented with his life, notwithstanding the considerable misfortunes he had suffered. It was, after all, the fate of Man to have to accept what he could no longer change. Tonala felt there was little else he could do to improve the lives of his family and tribesmen. He was chief of the feared and respected Sasquatchoni, and - as befitted his status - he lived in the biggest lodge in the village. He sat now with his back against an upright post in the crowded lodge and relaxed. His family and friends surrounded him as they recounted stories of past coups. Amid the hullabaloo of noise, broken occasionally by uproarious laughter, his new daughter, Concilla, was sitting quietly, combing his wife's hair.

Tonala watched her appreciatively. He looked at the old sub-chief sitting beside him, and with a gesture at Concilla said: "She is a good woman - RoShann has chosen well. I wonder what success he is having at the council of tribal chiefs in the north?"

Tamayo, a wise old warrior of unknown age, set aside his pipe, and replied: "I think he will impress them. He told me he feels very proud to be representing the tribe at such an important gathering."

"Yes, Tamayo – that is why I gave him the honour. One can grow strong with responsibility, I…"

Tonala stopped speaking. His eyes narrowed and he turned his head sideways to listen. He waved his arms to request the attention of the others. "Silence!"

A distant rumbling sound was growing louder. Now they could all hear the staccato reports of gunfire.

"Into the darkness," he commanded. "Hurry!"

The frightened women gathered their children as the men rushed outside to grab their weapons. Reaching for his rifle, Tonala pulled aside the buffalo robe covering the lodge entrance and plunged through.

In the faint moonlight he quickly ascertained that the camp was being attacked from two directions. Without taking aim, he fired at the oncoming troopers until his rifle was empty. A charging horse caught him with its quarter, sending him sprawling to the ground. He regained his feet and retrieved his rifle. Using it as a club, he smashed it against the head of a nearby soldier. Drawing his knife, he threw himself at the raiders, slashing at their soft flesh. Bloodcurdling screams pierced the night as his blows found their target. He looked for another enemy and raced towards a young trooper; he could see fear written on his opponent's face. The soldier raised his arm and aimed his revolver as the chief was almost upon him. Before Tonala could strike, the gun exploded.

Somehow, the hooves of the milling horses missed him. Blinded, his head wound throbbing and burning, Tonala struggled to stand. He knew what had to be done: *'Fight until your head dies!'* He felt weak and tired and desperately wanted to lie down. Shaking his head, he tried to focus his eyes. There was no sensation of movement when he walked, but his dying spirit found new impetus in the cries of the women and children around him. They were being slaughtered...

Colonel Austin stood before him, clutching the reins of his horse. He pointed his gun at Tonala, but the nervous dance of the animal deflected his aim. Wounded again, Tonala staggered. Drawing on his deep reserves of determination, he continued to move towards the colonel.

Austin spun the cylinder of his gun as the hammer repeatedly clicked on empty chambers. With a panicked inflection rising in his voice, the colonel screeched out: "Shoot him, somebody! Shoot that damned Indian!"

Such was his fear and detestation of the Sasquatchoni, his limbs were frozen with horror as the huge, bloodied figure of Tonala stumbled towards him.

"Cut him down, don't let him touch me! Damn you to Hell, shoot 'im!"

Austin threw the useless handgun at Tonala, just as the Sasquatchoni chief lunged at him. Clutching the colonel in a bear-like embrace, Tonala began dragging his adversary over to the fiercely burning lodge. Amidst the chaos and confusion, no one seemed to notice that Austin was being carried away. The heat of the flames began to singe the white man's hair as he was pushed back into the inferno. His feet tripped on burning timbers and he cried out in terror.

Suddenly, there was a loud crack and Tonala faltered as a bullet passed through his body. His dying gasp sprayed the colonel's face with blood.

Major Stevens lowered his rifle and watched as the giant Indian chief slowly collapsed on top of the colonel.

Austin was winded and trapped beneath Tonala's dead body. He looked into the chief's hawk-like face. Tonala's open eyes stared back at him accusingly, and the corpse still gripped him in its lifeless arms.

With his voice full of loathing, Colonel Austin yelled out: "Get this stinking Indian off o'me!" The nearest troopers ran to help him up. Anxious to leave, he grabbed a loose horse and raced off into the night.

The speed of the attack caused total confusion among the Sasquatchoni. With no chief to command them they abandoned their camp. Those that escaped the burning lodges were ruthlessly gunned down: men, women and children. For good measure, the colonel ordered that even the tribe's livestock should be systematically destroyed.

* * * *

Riding easily along the trail O'Hara allowed himself a

little smile. "Yes sir, I owe that to nobody but myself."

He was pleased that his negotiations with the corn exchange had gone smoothly. The gold had helped in that, of course. He had managed to swing a deal with the wholesaler and keep his promise to the Indians. Now, he rode beside three wagons loaded with corn, accompanied by enough horses and teamsters to drive them out of town.

After several hours of following dirt trails the party had travelled the agreed distance towards the Black Hills. O'Hara raised a hand to call a halt to the wagons. It was time to pay the men off.

"Okay, boys, that's far enough. You can leave the wagons here with me. I got ten dollars a man for all of you." As he spoke, he reached inside his tunic for the money.

Before he could find his wallet one of the hired riders, a fat man who seemed to speak for the others, replied: "Yeah, sure, that's right major. But while we're here, we may as well take the rest of your money, too!"

O'Hara winced as a rifle was jammed viciously into his ribs.

"Y'see, me and the boys have talked it over. Don't try to haggle with us!" He spat on O'Hara's dusty boot. "We're also disputing the ownership of these here wagons

- ain't that right, boys?" This time he jabbed the rifle into O'Hara's neck.

"Be reasonable, major. We don't want any arguments." He spoke the words with an air of finality. "There's six of us, an' only one of you!"

"I don't need to pick an argument with you, fat man. Look!" O'Hara nodded his head at the Sasquatchoni warriors emerging from the brush.

As the ringleader turned his head to see what he meant, O'Hara's fist smashed into his jaw in a venomous, full-bodied punch. The fat man sprawled on the ground and O'Hara snarled at him: "I don't take kindly to having a rifle stuck in my ribs!" He massaged the bruised knuckle of his right hand and addressed the others: "I suggest you saddle tramps take that barrel of axle grease with you an' git!"

Having left the wagons with Mayat and his warriors, O'Hara made his way back to Fort Kearny. By late afternoon he needed a rest from the rigors of the trail. He found a secluded spot in which to make a fire and was busy gathering brushwood when he noticed an old prospector about to light a fire of his own. After an exchange of greetings O'Hara offered to add his kindling to the old man's supply in return for a cup of coffee. The old man went one better and stewed up some beans as well.

O'Hara gave a satisfied smile. "D'you know, old'un - you make the sweetest cup of coffee this side of South Dakota."

"Is that a fact? I always was open to flattery, son."

The hot black liquid scorched O'Hara's mouth, but it helped to wash away the trail dust.

"That was good. I'm obliged to you," he said.

Lowering the coffee pot the old man placed it back on the dying embers. "Let me fill yuh again, son."

O'Hara looked at the ragged, dust-covered clothing the old man was wearing. His hat had seen better days and there were crudely sewn repair patches on his boots and saddle gear. Oddly, the prospector's face was clean-shaven.

The old man caught O'Hara's gaze and rubbed his fingers across his jaw making a rasping sound. "I still make the effort – every other day."

"Having a hard time?" O'Hara enquired.

"Yep, an' it's gonna git harder, son. Yuh goddam soldier boys made sure o'that!" There was a hint of bitterness in his words.

O'Hara gave a puzzled frown. "How come?"

The old man scratched his head. "Yuh telling me, yuh don't know?"

O'Hara continued to drink his second cup of coffee and shook his head.

The prospector took a bite out of his tobacco plug and rolled the wad around in his mouth. He gazed thoughtfully at the fire before squirting a mouthful of brown liquid at it. The spittle splashed into the flames and sizzled. Standing up quickly, he said: "Yuh know what? I might just stay alive a couple o'more days!" Hurriedly, he kicked dirt over the fire.

"What the hell you rambling on about old man?" said O'Hara impatiently.

"So yuh ain't heard?"

"I've been traveling with a prairie breeze fanning my whiskers for a couple of days," said O'Hara.

"Well, two nights back I was taking a breather on a ridge just above the Sasquatchoni village…"

The old man spent the next hour relating in great detail the events he had witnessed, exactly as they had unfolded: "And from the darkness they poured in shot after shot, it was a massacre!" He stared at the cold, dead fire, shaking his head. "Yuh soldier boys sure 'nough chewed them up!"

O'Hara was visibly shaken by the statement. He sat still, his shoulders and jaw sagging as he stared at the dead fire.

Suddenly, he stood up and went over to his horse. He rummaged in his saddlebag, looking for his new fountain pen and a piece of paper. After searching for a few moments, he sat down and started to write.

O'Hara had been riding hard since leaving the old prospector's camp; now his horse was rolling and blowing. He was impatient to make progress, but he knew that if he didn't stop soon his horse would be knackered.

"Whoa, son - take it easy." Patting and stroking the horse's neck he dismounted, groaning at the aching pain in the back of his legs. Easing the cinch, he continued talking to the animal as he led the way along the trail. Eventually, he was within sight of his destination.

As he passed through the gates of Fort Kearny, O'Hara remained in control of his emotions. He did not acknowledge any greetings, nor return any salutes. He tied his weary horse to a hitching post and walked up the steps to Colonel Austin's quarters. Without knocking, he opened the door.

The noise of the slamming door surprised the colonel. He had just turned away from studying a wall map. In defiance of all army etiquette, O'Hara gave his superior officer a cold, hard look.

"It's customary to knock, major!" said the colonel,

now seated behind his desk.

O'Hara strode forward and stopped.

"For what you've done I should knock your bastard head off!"

"Aha, from your choice of words I take it you have been informed of my action against the Sasquatchoni - and of course you don't approve. Welcome back!"

O'Hara rested his knuckles on top of the desk and stared down at the seated colonel. He was unable to contain his anger any longer: "A welcome from you, I don't need, you yellow-dog sonofabitch!" He spat the words out bitterly.

The colonel was stung by O'Hara's insolence. Fuming with indignation he sprang to his feet, sending his mahogany chair crashing against the wall.

"How dare you! Why – why, you stupid Irish fool! What dung heap of a cattle boat did they throw you off of? I could have you court martialled for this…" his mind groped for the appropriate words, "for this gross insubordination!"

"Yeah, maybe you could. But we both know you won't, colonel. Too many awkward questions would be asked and you'd have to give evidence to justify what you've done," O'Hara replied sardonically.

Colonel Austin's lips broke into a thin smile as he

adopted a more civil manner. "*Touché*, major. It seems we understand each other – a little."

"Understand? No, colonel - not if I live to be a hundred!"

"You know very well why I took the action I did, major. It was common knowledge among the tribes that they could barter with the Sasquatchoni for their winter supplies. They had no need for the agency – or, for that matter, the reservation. With a hard winter in prospect there is now nowhere an Indian can go in order to survive, but the reservation!" Colonel Austin uttered his final sentence with an exultant gleam in his eyes.

"Do you understand that, major?" Austin's voice took on a plaintive tone as though he wanted O'Hara to concede that his reasoning was correct. "Once the tribes in this area accept that the reservation is their new home they will relinquish all right to future settlement on this land. The Sasquatchoni had to be destroyed."

O'Hara shook his head in disbelief. "Colonel, I disagree with your diagnosis and your methods. Before this is finished a lot of innocent people are gonna die! You've got to hope things go the way you planned - but I doubt you'll get much sleep at night. You've destroyed a unique people, along with their culture. You've taken a high stakes risk for the sake of your career; but I've got news for you, colonel: the dice are still rolling."

O'Hara looked intently at the colonel. "Don't you realize what you've done man? After this massacre the remaining Sasquatchoni will form an alliance with the other tribes, just as they did against Custer!"

The colonel made great play of pouring himself a small whiskey, before replying: "Major, the Sasquatchoni will do no such thing. They've been traders for a long time - far too long."

He let out a deep sigh and scratched the side of his nose as he deliberated the matter. Turning to O'Hara with a half-smile on his face, he said: "From this moment in time, major, I doubt the Sasquatchoni could muster enough warriors to hunt a three-legged buffalo - should one ever be found!"

The smile on the colonel's face was like barbed wire twisting in O'Hara's gut. "As I've always suspected," he said, "you're a bigoted fool." Raising his right arm he pointed in the direction of the prairie. "God damn it! Out there are three thousand Indians on the warpath, an' all you have is a hundred troopers at your disposal!"

"Indeed, major, I am aware of all the relevant facts. But they need not concern you."

Opening a drawer in his desk the colonel withdrew some documents and laid them face-up in front of O'Hara.

"These are your orders. You are to report to Fort Williams on transfer."

"Yeah, that figures. Fort Williams is two hundred miles away from here. How very convenient for you. So that's your trump card, colonel? Just as a matter of interest, who is to be my replacement?"

"Major Stevens," said the colonel, brusquely.

"Sure it is - who else could it be!" O'Hara shook his head. "Four days ago he made captain. Don't bother to explain, colonel. Everybody gets paid for services rendered. He's your kinda man: a glory hunting asshole!"

Having both had their say they glared fiercely at each other. Each man remained confident that he had won the encounter.

O'Hara turned around in disgust, but stopped on reaching the door. He looked back at Colonel Austin, pulled an envelope from his pocket and flicked it carelessly on top of his transfer papers. "Read it! I've resigned my commission. Like you say, colonel - *Touché!*"

Tipping his hat in a mock salute, he rasped: "You always were a lousy poker player!"

He left the room, slamming the door shut behind him.

THE DEATH OF INNOCENCE

* * * *

RoShann had no warning, no mental conception of the carnage and devastation that would greet his eyes as he approached the craggy bluff. The elevated position provided him and his band of twenty warriors with a sweeping, panoramic view of the prairie below - the hunting grounds of the Sasquatchoni where the tribe's main encampment was situated.

The warriors were all looking forward to returning home to the warm greetings of their family and friends. They could picture the laughter of their children as they raced to meet them with an assortment of dogs snapping at their heels.

RoShann dragged on the bridle of his big stallion and it responded immediately, slowing to a halt amid the rocky terrain. Now, all of the warriors could see the flat plains and beyond. There was no noise, no bustle - but instead, a stunning stillness. When they saw the blackened ground of their burned-out lodges their minds were filled with a sense of foreboding.

"The black crow that rested upon your shoulder this morning was an omen, RoShann," said one warrior.

Their young chieftain wasn't listening. Kicking and urging his frightened horse on, RoShann pulled savagely at its bridle and plunged recklessly down the steep incline.

Before reaching the perimeter of their camp they came across the first of many corpses. Recognizing the body of his wife, the leading warrior gave a fearful cry. He leapt from his horse as he called her name. The others left the bereaved warrior cradling the dead woman in his arms.

The other warriors began searching for their own families. Frantically, they ran from corpse to corpse.

A voice called out: "RoShann!"

He turned to see a powerfully built warrior walking slowly towards him, holding the dead body of his youngest son. "They are all dead!' said the warrior. "My family – gone!" He shook his head in bewilderment. As he looked down at his son's body he asked: "Who - and why? Who would kill our children?"

RoShann had no answer. He mounted his stallion and moved off in the direction of his father's lodge, trying hard to quell his anxiety.

Inside the lodge he found more bodies burned beyond recognition. "Concilla!" he called, suddenly afraid that he had lost her forever.

After a brief search he found the body of his father. Examining the corpse he counted the wounds. "Even you, Tonala, could not defeat the Great Spirit when he demanded your life." Overcome by a surge of sadness he sat, legs crossed, hands covering his face.

He recovered his composure and arranged the body of his father so that it lay in a manner befitting a great chief. As he did so, he found an army hat beneath it. The hat looked familiar.

A male voice singing in a toneless chant interrupted his thoughts.

RoShann retraced his steps around the numerous dead bodies that littered the ground. Ignoring the smell of putrefying flesh he stopped at a roofless, half-burnt lodge. His arrival disturbed a couple of coyotes, which slunk furtively away. Black crows and vultures squawked raucously, too gorged with human flesh to fly. He looked inside the structure.

"Tamayo! It is I, RoShann!" The old warrior took no heed of the voice and continued to look toward the Black Hills. A blanket was draped around his shoulders.

Tamayo was the oldest warrior of the tribe and had long been revered by the younger Sasquatchonis for his wisdom. Despite their affection, however, he was weary of his aches and pains and had often expressed his wish to die so that he might hunt with his ancestors. He had prayed to the Great Spirit many times for deliverance from life and could not understand why his simple wish had so far been denied to him. Now, he felt his life had been all but extinguished.

After a diligent search amongst the corpses he had managed to find all the members of his family. With a great physical effort he had somehow found the strength to carry the bodies back to his lodge. There, he had placed them all back in the positions they had customarily occupied in life.

He sat there now, with his eyes closed, softly mouthing a lament.

"Why, oh Great Spirit, why?
My family should be weeping for me
Not I for them!
Men must not be seen to cry
But we do, deep inside.
All life must end, but not like this!
Why?"

Tamayo moved his shoulders from side to side keeping pace with the rhythm of his sorrow. RoShann moved away, instinctively knowing that it would not be possible to communicate with the old warrior.

The sound of his name being called made him spin around. Recognizing the voice, he called out. "Concilla!

Where are you? Concilla!" He looked desperately about him to determine where the voice was coming from.

Emerging from between the lodges she called to him again: "RoShann!"

She dropped the water container she had been carrying and raced towards him, throwing herself into his arms. She held RoShann's face and showered him with kisses, trying hard to suppress her spontaneous tears. They clung to each other fiercely. RoShann waited, gently calming her fears and her babbling tongue.

He suspected he knew who was responsible for the killings, but he wanted confirmation. "What happened, Concilla? Who would dare to carry out such an attack on the Sasquatchoni?"

More stable and composed now, Concilla related the story of the massacre. When her account was finished, she said sadly: "Roshann, your mother is dying. The army major, your friend, has been helping us. Come!"

With O'Hara's help, Concilla had managed to build a wickiup that was just sufficient to accommodate her and RoShann's mother. As RoShann arrived at the shelter O'Hara was returning with some firewood. RoShann acknowledged his help with a nod of his head.

In the last couple of hours his mind had received shock after shock: and now this. Was he too late? He squeezed himself into the flimsy shelter.

His mother's face was wreathed about with her thick black hair. Her skin was cold and pale. RoShann thought it strange that with death so near she could look so beautiful. He stared at her, his mind numb. A nudge from Concilla brought him back from the realm of self-pity. Kneeling, he examined the jagged wound in his mother's side. He laid his head on her breast and listened to her heartbeat.

He was aware of her fingers gently caressing the hair on the back of his head. They clutched at him with failing strength. He leaned forwards to hold her hand and pressed his lips to her face. Suddenly, her eyes opened wide. Her lips moved, soundlessly calling his name. After a few moments, she fell into a deep sleep.

RoShann left the wickiup and walked over to the major.

"Your mother?" asked O'Hara.

"She breathes, but is like the dead. By morning her spirit will be gone."

"I'm sorry," said O'Hara. "I keep on questioning myself. If I had been at Fort Kearny that day, I swear to you, this would never have happened."

"I believe you, my friend. Do not blame yourself. Colonel Austin is an ambitious man, full of hatred for the Sasquatchoni. He found a way to strike in your absence.

While you were buying corn, he was planning war. But you risk your life here, major. There are those amongst us who would not see a white man in our camp. Over a hundred people of my tribe are now dead!"

"Yes, I know," replied O'Hara. "Because of this -" he waved his arm to indicate the devastated camp, "I've resigned my commission. I'm just waiting for the confirmation to arrive. Then I'm a free agent."

"Will you not miss being a soldier?" enquired RoShann.

"Yeah, I guess I will. It's been my life. But I've applied for the post of Commissioner of Indian Affairs in this territory. If things go my way, I'll still be around."

Walking over to his horse, O'Hara swung himself up into the saddle.

"Colonel Austin has transferred me to Fort Williams. Right now I'm still on the army payroll, so I have to report."

"Fort Williams is many days ride from here, is it not?"

O'Hara nodded his head.

"Good!' exclaimed RoShann. He stared hard into O'Hara's eyes. "There, you will be safe. I would not like to be responsible for your death!"

Holding Colonel Austin's hat in his hand, he glanced at it and said: "This soldier has been shown much respect by our chiefs. But in the days that follow he will come to learn why the Sasquatchoni are feared by the other tribes!" The quiet assertion was full of hidden menace.

With a contemptuous flick of his arm he sailed the hat away from him.

O'Hara was not surprised at RoShann's desire for vengeance. It was inevitable that he would now assume authority as chief of the tribe. Looking at him, O'Hara could see that the tragedy had made him grow in stature. He took note of the flaring nostrils and the clamped jaw as RoShann controlled his anger before speaking.

"By this one callous act, Colonel Austin has breeched the dam and released the waters from the river. Now, it will flow in all directions - changing to blood!"

O'Hara was left to stare at the broad back of the young Indian chief as he walked away, the stark, chilling words echoing though his brain.

RoShann knew he had much to do. The survivors of the tribe had apparently retreated to a canyon, where they were sheltering in the caves. It was a two-day ride from the destroyed encampment.

Concilla touched his arm. "Listen, RoShann! The chanting has stopped!"

They hurried over to Tamayo's desolate lodge and

found him dead. He was lying amongst the blood-spattered bodies of his family. He had cut his own throat.

RoShann closed the dead man's eyelids with a brush of his fingers. "You have set your spirit free, Tamayo. Now you can rest."

Running to his horse, RoShann called to Concilla: "I must go to the canyon!"

His mind was made up: he would shame his people out of their apathy and bring them back to bury their dead.

9. VENGEANCE

Native American mythology holds that when the Great Spirit created the world he divided it into the darkness of night and the bright light of day. For the first time man could see man: friendships could be forged, or wars fought. Human history has been punctuated by wars and alliances ever since.

During the American Civil War between the North and the South, brother fought brother and fathers killed sons. Many lessons were learned. Ultimately, Abraham Lincoln gained a measure of emancipation for the black slaves; but for the so-called 'Red Indian' - the true American - there was to be no relief from persecution.

RoShann, Chief of the Sasquatchoni was bitter and sought revenge for the injustices his tribe had suffered.

Under his charismatic leadership the tribe's warriors ranged far and wide spreading fear amongst the white settlers of South Dakota Territory. When an alarm was raised amongst the homesteads it was often preceded by a cry of: *"It's the Sasquatch!"* The tall, muscular figures of the Sasquatchoni men were easily identifiable as they executed their carefully planned ambushes against army patrols. Before carrying out their attacks they would destroy all nearby telegraph lines to hinder the army's lines of communication.

Although Colonel Austin had been severely censured by the army's High Command for perpetrating the Sasquatch massacre without authorization, he had subsequently been detailed to prevent uprisings within the area under his command. He continued to believe that his actions would be vindicated in the long term.

Clearing his throat, he addressed a patrol before it left Fort Kearny: "I want to remind you men: no prisoners are to be taken! Remember: this war is about survival – it's them or us. Besides, we have no room for vermin in Fort Kearny. Now, we all know that bullets cost money; but if it takes six shells to bring down one Sasquatch it will be money well spent! Carry on, lieutenant!"

The Sasquatchoni warriors paid the price of his policy with their lives.

Slowly, the seasons changed. For once, the winter approached grudgingly, spreading its chill shadows over high land, but leaving the plains free of frost. The sun was still warm, abated by a cooling breeze. In wooded areas the trees stood forlorn and bare; their branches resembled bony fingers reaching upwards to clutch the scurrying snow clouds.

Major Tim O'Hara's resignation from the army had been accepted with protest and regret. But his simultaneous application for the office of Commissioner of Indian Affairs had been successful. Though new to the post, by means of patient negotiation he had managed to persuade some of the tribes that the more fertile reservations would be good places for their families to live.

An old Indian saying insisted that a burning hatred should either be quickly acted on, or forcibly forgotten. If left to fester, an unexpended hatred could cause a man to lose his appreciation of the many beautiful things in the world. RoShann could neither forgive nor forget. Indeed, his mind was consumed by one thought: How to kill Colonel Austin, before the army under his command completely annihilated the Sasquatchoni...

* * * *

As the autumn daylight began to fade the captain and his men returned from their patrol. They rode up to Fort Kearny, its walls bathed in a golden glow, its doors opened wide in welcome. Every man on the patrol was glad to return to the sanctuary of the fort, to obtain some respite from the sharp winds. Obeying the dictum that a cavalryman's first duty is to his horse, the troopers stripped off their saddle-gear and headed straight for the corral to work on the remuda.

The officers saluted a passing column until the last man had gone by, then hitched their mounts to the post outside Colonel Austin's office. When the column had disappeared, they performed a smart about-face and went inside to make their reports.

An hour later, two troopers were patrolling the main gates on sentry duty. They stamped their feet repeatedly, as much to alleviate their boredom as to fend off the cold - but it helped to restore their circulation, nonetheless. The big gates of the fort were still open. The evening temperature had begun to drop rapidly and the first chill winds of the early fall were rolling in from the prairie flat lands. The air was laden with autumnal odors.

"It's gettin' cold Zack!" said the young soldier as he tugged at the collar of his cloak. "Y'know what I'd like now - to keep me warm?"

Zack laughed quietly to himself and replied: "Sure I do, Sonny: a big hot fart!"

"Ho hum, ain't you the funny one!"

"Okay..." Zack relented, "how 'bout this: you'd like the finest bottle of malt whiskey!'

Slowly shaking his head from side to side, Sonny replied: "John Barleycorn? Nah... what I'd like is one of those Cheyenne women!"

"Oh, you would, huh! Listen, Sonny - you horny little bastard - you wouldn't know what t'do with it. Before you could whistle 'Dixie' she'd cut off your balls - and you'd be the funny one."

A muffled noise outside the fort interrupted Zack's diatribe.

"Oh, hell - what was that?" His face creased in irritation.

"Stop yapping will ya," said Sonny. "The wind's knifing through here. Let's close the gates!"

"Hold it, Sonny - listen!" The young trooper strained his eyes, trying to peer into the darkness. "It looks like the patrol left somebody behind!"

They could hear hoof beats approaching the gates. A figure on horseback slowly emerged from the gathering dusk, heading for the main entrance. In the flickering torchlight Zack could just discern that the rider was an officer. In an automatic gesture he swung him a salute.

"Nearly shut you out that time, lieutenant!" he said.

There was no reply. With its ears pricked the officer's horse gave a snort and plodded sedately towards its companions at the hitching post.

When the rider and his mount had gone inside the compound, Zack turned to Sonny in indignation. He was offended at the officer's snub. "Did you see that? That stiff-necked jackass ignored me. He didn't even have the good manners to return my salute! Maybe he thinks I ain't good enough. Jeez!'

"Yeah, so I noticed. Times are getting bad in this man's army, Zack."

"You can bet your boots on that, kid," said Zack, somewhat mollified by Sonny's assessment. "Did you see what he was carrying under his cloak? It was quite a package, whatever it was." Sonny's voice rose in pitch as he exclaimed in mock excitement: "Say! You don't think he's hiding one o'them Cheyenne girls d'you, huh?"

Zack turned around slowly, hands on hips. "Can't you raise that pea-sized brain of you'rn above a woman's fanny?" He shook his head in disbelief.

"Hold on, Zack: look over there - he's still mounted."

Both troopers were now filled with curiosity. The late arrival had not left his horse. He sat astride it, ramrod straight, as though he was waiting for someone to assist him.

"D'you think he's taken sick?" said Sonny.

"I don't rightly know," said Zack. "Let's go over and see what he wants."

Ignoring the open gates, they ambled across to the silent rider, unsure of his rank or attitude.

"You okay, sir?" ventured Zack.

There was no reply, so the two moved closer.

"Um, are you injured, sir? Can we help you dismount?"

Tentatively, Zack began to lift the edge of the officer's cloak. Beneath it, the dim light shed by his torch revealed that the man's hands had been tied to the saddle horn. Then he noticed that the rider's eyes were not blinking.

He felt the hair on the back of his neck raise up.

"Hey, Sonny - get the first sergeant. Move your ass boy, we got ourselves a dead man here!"

Zack and Sonny's attention was completely focused on the dead rider, so they did not notice a wagon being moved into position outside the gates. Four Sasquatchoni warriors quickly ran to their stations. One pulled up the side covers and readied the belts of ammunition, while RoShann lined up the Hotchkiss machine gun through the open gates: the other two warriors held the blindfolded horses steady.

News of the mounted corpse and its unexplained appearance spread rapidly around Fort Kearny. Troopers in various states of dress drifted out in twos and threes, until it seemed as though the entire strength of the fort had filled the compound.

"Is he one of ours?" said a trooper.

"What d'you think, bonehead? Of course he's one of ours!"

"Say, its an officer!" shouted a voice from the front.

"Why - if it ain't Patterson!"

"It's the best thing that could have happened to that bastard," said a rueful young recruit. An older soldier standing next to him immediately punched the youngster on the side of his face.

"Hey! What was that for?" exclaimed the stunned trooper as he picked himself out of the horseshit, rubbing his bruised jaw.

"Keep your meat-hole shut, pal; he was a nice kid!"

Patterson had only joined the company recently and

was not known to many of the men. But it remained their duty to show respect for an officer, even though they had grown callous in the face of death over the past few weeks.

They were all curious to know what the package beneath the rider's cloak contained. It appeared to be strapped to his back.

"It's gotta be booze," suggested a voice from the back.

"Sure it is, he wanted us to see him off in the right way!" Somewhere in the crowd, a trooper sniggered self-consciously.

A shaft of yellow light cutting through the darkness made the sergeant call the troopers to order. Silhouetted in the doorway was Colonel Austin. He had been disturbed by the ruckus and ribald comments and was determined to restore order. He moved along the verandah followed by his senior officers. His thin, sarcastic voice pierced the cool night air, devoid of any warmth: "Hell and damnation, sergeant! What is going on here? What is the cause of this indiscipline?" He spat the words out rapidly, hardly able to contain his anger. "When you can find the time, sergeant, perhaps you will be kind enough to keep your commanding officer informed!"

"Begging the colonel's pardon, but we have a dead man here, sir!"

"Well - who is it?"

"It's Lieutenant Patterson, sir."

"Oh! That's too bad, dammit!" Austin gripped the rail outside his office, his knuckles whitening. "But if he's dead, how come he's sitting in the saddle? Who brought him in?"

"Nobody, sir, he came in on his own. He was tagged on the end of the detail."

"There's something wrong here, colonel," said Major Stevens, nervously.

"Yes, Jack, I agree. Patterson's patrol isn't due back until tomorrow. Where are the others? Apart from them, we have the whole company assembled here."

Slowly, he looked around the fort. His mind was racing, struggling to understand what had occurred. He was by nature a suspicious man, and he was suddenly filled with alarming thoughts.

"Sergeant! Maintain discipline! Shut the men up and get them back to their quarters. Something about this doesn't smell right! Sentries! Back to your posts! ...And close the goddam gates! Sergeant, put those men on a charge: 'dereliction of duty'!"

Major Stevens was looking closely at the dead rider. "What's that he's carrying behind him sergeant?" he enquired.

"I'm just gonna check it out, major."

Pulling aside the dead lieutenant's cloak, the puzzled sergeant reported: "Why - it's two barrels of gunpowder, major!"

At that moment, Colonel Austin had a sudden premonition of what was going to happen. He realized he had fatally underestimated the Sasquatchoni.

"No! It can't be!" he gasped.

At this startled utterance from their commanding officer, the troopers froze.

The colonel yelled hysterically: *"The gates! That's it, close the gates!"*

Running forward he kicked at the dead rider's horse; his lips worked furiously shouting urgent commands.

The staccato blast of the machine gun cut angrily through the night, peppering the compound with bullets. Sonny and Zack were the first to fall as they ran back to their post.

Within seconds, an enormous explosion had shattered the orderly calm of Fort Kearny. A huge ball of orange flame roiled and expanded over the parade ground, bringing a sudden hellish glow to the scene. The blast destroyed all the nearby buildings and set fire to many others. Torn and shredded bodies fell from the air like broken twigs to lay in grotesque positions on the scorched ground. A shower of fire arrows set ablaze the tinder dry wooden structures of any buildings that remained standing.

The machine gun chattered insatiably until there was no further movement inside the compound.

Their task completed, the handful of warriors waited for RoShann.

RoShann knew his band of avengers would not be pursued immediately. It would take time for news of the devastation of Fort Kearny to reach other white settlements and for them to organize tracking operations.

In the meantime, there was an important ritual to perform. He and the warriors who had accompanied him dismounted and walked slowly towards the tribal burial ground. The other surviving Sasquatchoni were already gathered together at the sacred site. The fire beneath Tonala's platform was burning fiercely.

RoShann stood before them and pointed towards the Black Hills as he bade farewell to his father: "Go now, Tonala! Go, my father! You are free! Your spirit need not remain earthbound. Ride into the sky. It is done: your soul is avenged. Go, I say!"

Holding the shaft of Tonala's war lance high, he plunged it forcefully into the red earth.

As the fire burned away the corner posts of the

platform it suddenly collapsed and the corpse crashed into the fiery furnace. A shower of sparks soared upwards into the dark night.

Some of the warriors present later swore on a sacred oath that they had seen Tonala's spirit rise up on its way to the heavenly hunting grounds. It was a story they would tell and retell.

There was much joy and celebration amongst the members of the tribe when the warriors returned to the caves in the canyon. After spending some time describing what had taken place at Fort Kearny, RoShann heard his name being called. He looked over his shoulder to see who it was, then smiled as he recognized his friend, Mayat. They clasped arms in salutation.

"Did your plans succeed?" asked RoShann.

"Where, once, there were wooden houses – now, there are none. Stampeding cattle have no respect for a white man's village…"

Fires burned long into the night as individual warriors related their stories. When all had been heard, and congratulations exchanged, the women gathered to cook celebratory meals.

But RoShann was uneasy. He sighed wearily; now

that Colonel Austin was dead he had no desire to continue the war. It was not possible in any case; the Sasquatchoni were so depleted, it had to end.

A slow wind caressed him as he walked alone through the shadows at the bottom of the canyon; the boulders stood around him like sentinels in the moonlight as he contemplated the tribe's predicament. He felt he had become one with the earth that supported him. His mind was fatigued from pondering the same, unanswered questions: *"How can the Sasquatchoni survive? Where can we go?"*

He had, at most, five days to reach a conclusion, before the army's Indian scouts discovered the tribe's whereabouts. He glanced at the full moon as it bathed the canyon in its silver light and whispered to himself: "If we are trapped here, the army will slaughter us all – down to the last woman and child!"

On the third day he decided that his people would have to leave the canyon and camp down in the old Indian ruins on top of the mesa – at least, for a while.

The Spanish Conquistadors had been the first outsiders to discover the Pueblo Indians' well-planned villages. The friendly Pueblo peoples had suffered much persecution at the hands of the Spanish, and had eventually been driven to seek refuge on the imposing, high-topped plateau, some five hundred feet above the surrounding terrain. They had long since abandoned the settlement, and it was now derelict. Nevertheless, it had the advantage that it could be easily defended by a small group of determined warriors, should that become necessary. This was to be the Sasquatchonis' new camp.

10. FLIGHT TO SAFETY

Calling a halt at noon, RoShann was thankful for the meal Concilla had prepared for him.

"Eat RoShann! You, above all of us, must keep up your strength. We need you to lead us!"

RoShann smiled wanly and looked at Concilla. "You are a good wife," he replied. "I chose wisely. But I did not mean our life together to be like this."

He reached out and touched her face. "Perhaps I was wrong to take you from your homeland..." Holding his hand to her face, Concilla answered: "I would have died if you had not taken me with you, RoShann... I would have died!"

He drew her close to him and they kissed tenderly. He held her tightly as he tasted the salt sadness of the tears on her face.

She hesitated, then spoke again: "RoShann, could we not... could we not take what is left of our tribe to the high valley in the mountains? We might be safe there..."

He nodded. "I, too, have been thinking of the valley. It is a difficult journey and some of us may not be strong enough to survive it. But we must try to get there. Every day, more and more white men arrive here to take possession of our land." He paused to look at the small surviving remnant of the once feared and respected Sasquatchoni tribe. "Soon, there will be nothing left of our people. When we make camp on the mesa, I will inform the tribe about our true destination. Come, let us ride."

It took little time for the Sasquatchonis to make themselves at home in the pueblo ruins. For the first time in weeks the warriors and their families lived as a tribe should. They repaired the old adobe houses, told stories - danced, loved and laughed with each other. They hunted and found just enough food to abate their hunger. If they were worried about the shortage of things to eat, they tried not to show it. Despite their happy faces, however, it was plain to everyone that there was nothing to stow away for the long winter months ahead.

RoShann called for a council to discuss the tribe's plight. On the morning of the meeting the people went about gathering their firewood as the first light snows of winter began to fall. A few weathered timbers from a ruined adobe made a good fire in one of the larger dwellings. As they sat around it, everyone could feel its cheering heat. The older members of the tribe sat closest to the fire, hugging its warmth.

There was a respectful silence as people entered the building and arranged themselves around the room until, at last, it was full.

RoShann rose from his seated position to address the throng. As he did so, his tall physique towered over them.

Before he could begin, a warrior exclaimed: "Chiefs of the Sasquatchoni have always spoken true words to their people. We would have it no other way, RoShann!"

Another voice added: "We are not afraid RoShann! Whatever you demand of us, will be done!"

RoShann was gratified by the show of support as he raised his hands to signal that they should be quiet. The tribe's situation was dire and unsustainable. They all knew that they could not survive the winter in the bleak pueblos and many had been praying to the Great Spirit for salvation. RoShann was now their only hope.

He began to speak in a low, clear voice: "My people, I want to talk to you about our past, present and future. Today we have eaten, our bellies are full, and we will sleep well tonight. But our warriors have returned from the hunt with nothing: so there will be little to eat tomorrow." He let the silence linger for a few moments. "The white men want us to live on a reservation. They say there is food and shelter there. But I know that you do not wish to live in a cage."

There was a murmur of agreement as all eyes looked expectantly at RoShann.

"We must be aware that whoever takes command of the soldiers in days to come, will want to impress his chief with a great victory over the mighty Sasquatchoni…"

Again, the people nodded their heads in agreement.

"You are wise enough to know that this place can be no more than a temporary shelter. It cannot feed us properly, and without food we will lose our strength. If we stay here, we will die. It is only a matter of time before we are found."

He paused for someone to suggest an alternative scenario: no voice was raised.

An old woman sitting near the fire tugged her shawl tightly around her shoulders. She yelled spiritedly: "Tell them, RoShann, tell them what to do! Speak, and they will follow you! The young need you to lead them to safety. The future of the tribe is theirs. As for myself, I have decided to stay here."

Impressed by the woman's courage, RoShann tilted his head slightly towards her and said:

"If that is your word, it shall be respected."

He closed his eyes momentarily and drew in a deep breath, then expelled the air from his lungs with a rush. His physical exhaustion and the weight of responsibility he carried showed on his face.

Concilla noticed his hesitation and called to him, her voice filled with concern: "RoShann! Are you unwell?"

He reassured her firmly. "No, Concilla – I am just a little tired." He straightened himself and continued: "My friends and fellow warriors, listen to me: I know of a land ten days from here, where we will find good hunting, fresh water - and no white men."

He circled the fire gazing silently at each member of his audience, challenging one of them to ask the next question. It came from Mayat.

"Where is this land you speak of, RoShann?"

Pointing towards the west, at the hills in the far distance, RoShann replied: "Over the mountains!"

There was a general movement of bodies as heads turned to look at each other, surprised at the improbability of the assertion. A babble of confused comment broke out between the men-folk as they shook their heads in disbelief.

Nayado, the oldest warrior present, could not recall anyone ever making the journey. He questioned RoShann further: "How could we climb the mountains – are they not always covered in snow? How could we survive the cold?"

The crackling of burning wood was the only sound to break the silence. All eyes were fixed on the young chief. The people waited patiently for RoShann to answer.

At his beckoning, Concilla came forward. Instead of standing behind him, as was the custom, she chose a position beside her husband. Reaching into his pouch, RoShann held aloft a peculiar, misshapen root.

"Only in the hunting grounds on the other side of the Snow Mountains can this herb be found!" he declared. He gave half of the red speckled root to Concilla and bit on the rest himself. The two of them began to chew the fibrous vegetable, reducing it to a pulp that they could wash down with some water. He spoke again: "Do you remember the day I returned to our camp with a cloak of feathers for Chief Tonala? I could not tell the whole story of my adventures, for there are times when secrets must be kept to protect others. But now, our own survival depends upon the truth being revealed..."

As they waited, RoShann told the tribe of his ascent of the Snow Mountains and his discovery of the hidden valley. He asked his audience not to be alarmed if he and Concilla began to change in appearance.

The warriors listened attentively; never had they

heard such a fantastic story. It was hard to believe, but it was intriguing and they listened obediently, with no interruptions. In accordance with their tradition, they passed their pipes back and forth as they absorbed the tale, smoking contentedly. A mother pushed her breast into her baby's mouth to stop it from crying. The listeners laughed as RoShann and Concilla began to undress in front of them – they could not understand why it was necessary. But in a short time, those people sitting closest to the fire began to blink and rub their eyes. Their senses insisted that an almost indiscernible change had taken place. Was it possible? RoShann and Concilla looked even bigger than before. Their limbs had begun to swell in size. Some of the onlookers blamed the smoke or bad tobacco.

All the tribe's people were suddenly aware that they were witnessing the transfiguration of RoShann and Concilla. It seemed the story was true - and they were suddenly afraid. Some of them pressed their faces to the ground to blot out the horror of what they were witnessing: others, stricken with fear, ran out of the adobe to hide from the abominations that were evolving before them. The majority of them sat, petrified - their eyes staring straight ahead, their mouths hanging open, afraid to take a breath. The monstrous forms taking shape in front of them were totally beyond their comprehension. They were hypnotized by the unnatural vision, and fascinated by what was occurring.

Working the spittle around his dry mouth, Mayat swallowed hard. His thoughts recoiled at the evidence of his eyes. *'This cannot be! A man and a woman's form cannot change simply by eating a root!'*

For the sake of his own sanity he reminded himself: *'But there is much in the world I do not understand: I do not know where the rain comes from, or why the sun disappears from the sky every night. Only the Great Spirit knows these things. We are as children before him: we accept his gifts and his judgement.'*

The only way to deal with his fear was to confront it. Mayat threw off his blanket. He strode forward and stood in front of the hideous apparitions his friends had become. With half-closed eyes he inspected their barely recognizable facial features.

"RoShann?" he enquired. "Is that you? Concilla?" He touched the thick, reddish-brown hair that covered their bodies. Only when RoShann spoke, was he convinced that his chief still stood before him.

"Now do you understand?" said RoShann. "This is how we will climb over the Snow Mountains!"

11. THE FORKED PATH

With the end of the Civil War the huge armies raised by both sides had to be disbanded. At a public ceremonial address the President thanked his commanders and the troopers of all ranks for their services, and urged them to return to whatever state they called home. They had to try to put together the broken pieces of their shattered lives.

In front of the House of Representatives, he spoke to the nation once again:

The President of the United States

"I would like to address the armies and the men of both sides of the recent conflict.

Most of you have medals or citations acknowledging your effort and valor on the field of battle. There were many who fought with courage and many who paid the ultimate sacrifice. There were no winners in the conflict between the North and the South. We all gave, and we all lost a little of ourselves.

We must not let those sacrifices be in vain!

We now have to prepare ourselves to fight another battle: the battle to rebuild this once great country, to restore its economy and prestige. It won't be easy to achieve. Anything worth fighting for never is.

We have colossal debts, gentlemen; and as a consequence, the future holds nothing but hard work for us all. However, this time we will fight our cause as one nation. Together, we can re-build our towns and forge our country into a great nation the whole world will respect.

Gentlemen: The United States of America."

The peacetime army of the reinstated Union numbered no more than fifty thousand men and they were very thinly spread over the country's enormous hinterland. News of the slaughter at Fort Kearny had shocked the generals in Washington. Reacting swiftly, they had assembled a company of six hundred troopers, mostly greenhorn youngsters and a few old veterans from every camp or fort that could spare a few men, and placed the unit under the command of General Morgan Wells. He was a Civil War veteran and long-time Indian fighter - a humane and intelligent man, with no desire for unnecessary bloodshed. His brief was to investigate what had occurred at Fort Kearny, to rebuild it as quickly as possible - and to pacify the local Indian tribes. On arriving at the devastated fort the first thing the general did was to send a letter to his old friend, Tim O'Hara.

"Well, what d'you think of that for a bean-feast, major?" Without waiting for a reply, the general continued: "I swear I've got myself the best goddam cook in this man's army, and no mistake! Of course, living out here I don't suppose you get to eat fine food very often. Would I be right in thinkin' that?" As he spoke he pushed himself away from the table and patted his copious stomach with satisfaction. Placing a large cigar between his teeth he adroitly nipped the end off and carefully enlarged the hole at the mouth-end. Then he struck a match and drew deeply, tasting the cool fumes at the back of his throat. As he slowly released the smoke, he experienced an acrid burning sensation in his nostrils, making him smile with delight.

O'Hara was staring at the roaring fire, feeling relaxed and at ease in the general's new quarters. Taking the pipe from his mouth he replied: "General, the food reminded me of you: the meat was as tough as a horse's hide and the apple pie, though hard and crusty on the outside, was pretty soft in the middle." He added quickly: "Oh, and - I'm just a 'mister' now, not a major!"

Both men chuckled at their good-natured goading. They had a mutual understanding of each other that went far beyond the formality of rank.

"Huh, Tim, if I thought for one moment you were serious about the food, why, I'd take that dern cook outside an' shoot him!" said the general as he refilled their glasses with brandy.

"Tim, I'll give it to you straight. I've been informed that you are now the appointed Indian agent around here, but I happen to know that you are also – correction, were - the best damned officer they ever had in this horse shit'n cavalry!"

O'Hara could not prevent his face breaking into a smile. "That's a back-handed compliment if ever there was one!" he said.

"I mean every word I say. Think about the advantages of my offer: rejoin the troop and I'll promote you to full colonel! Help me get this territory settled once an' for all! What do y'say?"

Holding his hand up in protest and with a rueful look on his face, O'Hara exclaimed: "Whoa, Morgan!" He reached over and threw another log on to the dying fire, then seated himself comfortably again before answering. "Had you approached me with that proposition a couple o'months ago, I would have said, 'yeah'. But now I think I can get the tribes a better deal as Superintendent of Indian Affairs."

"I'm sure you can... and will. Well, you can't blame an old man for trying, Tim. I was a little concerned when I heard about your resignation."

"I appreciate those words, Morgan," said O'Hara.

Picking up his brandy glass Wells ran his finger around the top, enjoying its fine smoothness. He flicked his middle finger gently against the rim.

"Listen to that!" He did it again. "Reminds me of how gracious life can be. My orderly takes great care of all my 'acquisitions'." He waved his arm around the room. "Over the years, my wife... bless her, has become a collector. The first thing she'll do when she arrives is to check over everything - and god help me if anything is broken!"

The general's eyebrows were furrowed together in an expression of concern. O'Hara, rocking in his chair, nodded his head in sympathy.

Wells continued: "Now you can see why my orderly is so indispensable! He holds the rank of sergeant, enjoys the traveling and the army way of life." His voice took on a more serious tone, as he got to the point: "You could have all that, and a lot more besides. One thing puzzles me, Tim: in all the years I've known you, you have never taken advantage of my position to further your own career. Y'know, you could have done yourself a lot of good, if you had used your friends more!"

O'Hara was swallowing the last of his brandy and on hearing the general's words he nearly choked. He rose from his chair; his stern features had set into a mask and his blue eyes gleamed coldly with indignation. "Morgan, you, of all people should know... that's never been my way! I won't lick any man's ass... not even yours!" He spoke slowly, emphasizing his words with a jabbing finger.

"Ha!" shouted the general, slamming his fist down on the table. "I knew that would get a rise out o'you!"

He stopped smiling. "Of course, I know you won't kowtow to anybody! Hell, if I said: *'kiss your own mother and in return I'll make you a general,'* you'd refuse - 'cause that's not the way a general should be made! You're a man of strong principles, Tim - that's what I like about you!"

Standing with his back to the fire, the general rubbed some warmth into his cold haunches. "You know why I'm here Tim? I've finally assembled my force of throw-outs. That is to say: my band of drunks and half-trained bogeyed recruits. With them - this company of rat bags - I'm supposed to rebuild Fort Kearny and round up any remaining Cheyenne, Shoshone and. Sioux Indians." He pulled each finger down savagely as he called out the tribes' names. "Oh, and I've also got to deal with the Comanche people, who are rampaging around the territory!"

O'Hara walked over to the fire. He knocked the ash from his pipe and studied the empty bowl before remarking idly: "You didn't mention the Sasquatchoni, Morgan. Have you forgotten about them?"

"On the contrary, Tim. You don't forget about a tribe that destroyed a trained cavalry outfit, no sir. So far, they've outsmarted everybody - including that pain in the ass, Colonel Austin." General Wells gritted his teeth in exasperation. "Oh, how I wish he'd survived - just so I could kick his balls off!"

"Have you ever seen the Sasquatchoni?" asked O'Hara.

"No, Tim, I never have."

"Well, sir - once seen, never forgotten. They're very tall." O'Hara stood upright to reveal his full six feet two inches of height. "Even I look up to them. They have a presence about them... a..." he hesitated, searching for the right word, "a magnificence. That's the only word I can think of to describe it."

"I'd imagine," said the general, "they might scare the living daylights out of someone who encountered them unexpectedly. I remember how impressed I was by your report about them."

Wells walked over to his desk and pulled open a drawer. Having found O'Hara's report, he began to read the words aloud:

Murder of a Nation

The U.S. Army recently carried out the mass slaughter of an Indian people known as the Sasquatchoni tribe. The Indians were ambushed at night and were mercilessly wiped out; indeed, the intention of the commanding officer in charge was to leave no survivors. To this end, as many Indian men, women and children as could be found were executed without trial. Even their dogs and horses were killed.

The intention of this unjust and bloody deed was to clear the land of Sasquatchoni influence, thus allowing it to be appropriated by white settlers.

Such an infamous and brutal act surely ranks as the most shameful ever perpetrated by an army unit and might be considered by some to be little more than murderous theft.

THE FORKED PATH

It is perhaps, an ironic twist of fate that the Sasquatchoni have been dispossessed by people who are themselves descendants of the dispossessed!

The general placed the thick folder down on top of his desk and frowned.

"I won't read it all, but I have to say, those words are seared into my mind. It's a good piece of writing – it goes to the heart of things. You may be interested to know, that the President happened to read my misplaced papers. It was he who set the wheels rolling here. Never been one for fancy words m'self."

O'Hara gave him a quizzical look.

"Ever thought of becoming a politician, Tim?"

The throwaway question surprised O'Hara. He hooked a thumb over his belt and replied: "That's a damn fool question to ask a man!"

General Wells nodded his head in agreement and tried unsuccessfully to hold back a smile. "It may not appeal to you now, but keep it in mind. Ultimately, all power resides in politics - not the barrel of a gun."

Walking over to a large map he gazed at it thoughtfully for a few moments.

"Ah, 'The United States of America'! How different it could have been for the Indians!"

Curious as to what the general meant, O'Hara went over to stand beside him. "In what way?" he enquired.

"That's a loaded question, Tim, but I'll try to answer it for you: a few years ago I came across a book, an early copy of Lewis and Clark's account of their expedition to Louisiana. It was written around the time Jefferson purchased the area from the French. Amongst a lot else, they listed all the tribes they'd ever had dealings with. That was... let me see... 1803, or thereabouts. The book says they head-counted over three thousand Indians. Since then, we've had a more detailed census performed."

Laying his swagger stick down, the general moved back to the comfort of the fire. "The figures suggest that six hundred thousand Indians hunted these prairie lands at one time or another! Well... if they had united under one leader and established a proper chain of command they could've..." He deliberately left the sentence unfinished.

"A nice idea Morgan, but not realistic," said O'Hara. "The tribes don't all speak the same language, so I don't see how they could have followed one man. And in any case, their pride wouldn't have let them form alliances with old enemies. That's not to say they lack the other things required to put up a fight – courage, determination, boldness."

Still holding his empty glass, Morgan Wells was lost in

thought as he savored the taste of the brandy.

He changed tack abruptly: "You do know, Tim, that I am under orders to arrest RoShann, the Sasquatchoni chief?"

"Yeah, I know," replied O'Hara. "That's Washington's way of being conciliatory."

"Is the Sasquatchoni tribe still a force to be reckoned with?" asked the general.

"No sir, they're not. As a fighting unit, they're finished. On Colonel Austin's orders no prisoners were taken. I guess there can't be too many survivors left." Knocking his pipe against the stone hearth, O'Hara watched the ashes disperse in the draught from the chimneystack. "They were never a big tribe: I don't think I ever saw more than about three hundred of them at any one time."

O'Hara sat down again and threw another log on the fire. "Those that remain alive will find the going pretty tough, that's for…"

A knock on the door interrupted the conversation. One of the general's staff lieutenants entered carrying a document case under his arm.

"You asked to see these directly, sir?"

"Yes I did, thank you, lieutenant."

The aide saluted and about-faced. When he had gone

the general picked up the newly arrived portfolio and let the papers flicker against his thumb.

Reluctantly, O'Hara pulled in his outstretched legs and rose to his feet.

"I think that's my cue for leaving, Morgan. The thickness of that pile o' paper means you'll be burning oil till midnight."

He shook the general's hand and thanked him for his hospitality before exiting. As he stepped through the door, General Wells gave him a final farewell slap on the back.

Outside, O'Hara immediately felt the cold air strike him. Standing alone for a few moments he shot a quick glance at the blackened ruins of the fort and saw the sentries huddling around their small fires. His body shivered involuntarily and he muttered a silent prayer, thankful that he didn't have to spend the night under canvas. With his shoulders hunched, he hurried along the walkway of the recently built block to his assigned quarters.

* * * *

The only indication that the adobe house was occupied was a thin curl of blue smoke that emerged from the air vent. It did not last long, as it was quickly whipped away by the fiercely blowing wind. The windows and door had been shuttered with heavy blankets in an attempt to retain some warmth.

Inside, Concilla watched distractedly as the sparks drifted slowly upwards. Suddenly, a piece of wood ignited and burst into flames, projecting the shadows of people lying around on the dirt floor.

The concord that had existed amongst the tribe had been broken. Their disconsolation was obvious; they had split into two groups: those who would follow RoShann; and those who had decided to stay behind because they were afraid of the strong medicine he had demonstrated to them. The latter group had no alternative plan to assist their survival and were now full of apathy and sorrow.

Concilla found her biggest bowl and filled it to the brim with hot soup – along with her share of the meat. RoShann knew it was useless to protest at her sacrifice; she was adamant that he needed it more than she did.

"You are twice the size of me, and a warrior!" she chided. Forcing the bowl into his hands, she walked back to the fire.

When everyone had eaten their own portion of food, they gathered together to discuss the events of the previous summer. It was painful for many to recall the recent past when, as a powerful tribe, they had possessed everything they needed. Now they had nothing.

"How many will follow your trail, RoShann?" asked Concilla, as she knelt on a blanket behind her husband.

He shook his head free of fire dreams before answering: "Only twenty." His big shoulders slumped with dejection. "We leave at daylight," he said.

Placing her arms around his neck so she could feel his body heat, she said: "And what of Mayat?"

"He will stay for two more days, to try to persuade the others to follow us. They are confused and afraid of change – and of the strange powers they have seen."

Concilla ran her fingers through RoShann's thick hair and massaged his shoulders. Playfully, she nibbled at the lobe of his ear, watching him twitch and smile. He stretched out on his back and began to relax. He looked into her eyes. "You are a good wife, Concilla."

The adobe was warm and the people were resting. Some were talking quietly, whilst others slept. In the flickering firelight, she could just see RoShann's face. Her cool palms soothed his forehead. With one finger, she traced the shape of his nose and lips. Gently, she ran her hands over his broad chest, squeezing and delicately pinching his flesh.

"I'm hungry, Concilla," whispered RoShann.

Though she understood the meaning of his words,

she admonished him, saying innocently: "But you have eaten! There is nothing more I can give you."

RoShann smiled, but would not be denied. Placing his hand against her thigh, he slowly and unrelentingly used his great strength to manipulate Concilla until she straddled his body. They kissed passionately as RoShann enjoyed the suppleness of Concilla's breasts. No one took any notice of the frantic movements beneath the blanket, or the quick intake of explosive breathing…

The chatter continued unabated, and a restless, whimpering, child was soon comforted.

* * * *

Pointing at the sky, the young warrior spoke as he nudged his horse closer. "Look RoShann! Manitou, the Great Spirit, has sent the sun to help us!"

A wintry glow had broken through the dark cumulus clouds, burning off the morning mist. Through gaps in the overcast layer they could see blue sky. Soon, the increase in temperature would melt the light covering of snow.

"It is a good omen - is it not, RoShann?" asked Concilla, as she looked back at the tabletop mesa and the friends she had been reluctant to leave.

"Yes, it is good for us!" he commented. As he spoke,

he noted that their tracks showed clearly in the friable earth. Shading his eyes against the brightness, he said, "Now we have gone, perhaps Mayat can persuade the others to follow us. We must hope they change their minds."

They had departed in the early dawn after an exchange of 'good luck' charms, tears and wailing laments. RoShann was satisfied with the distance his group had travelled during the morning as they tracked away from the mesa. He had only ever intended that it should be used as a temporary refuge and was acutely aware that it could become a death trap. It would only take three or four marksmen watching the trail for it to be effectively blockaded.

The build up of troopers at the fort had been reported to RoShann by his scouts. An indefinable instinct told him it was time to go. He knew the army could not afford to lose face after the Fort Kearny incident; its commanders would be more determined than ever now to sweep the plains clean of the red man. If, by some chance he were to be captured, he had no doubt they would make an example of him. There would be a public trial, a lot of political theatre, denunciations of the actions of the Indians and no comment at all about Colonel Austin's provocations. When it was over, the prosecution would demand a sentence of death by hanging. The remainder of the tribe would be resettled on an impoverished section of land - and the once-mighty Sasquatchoni would live in shame, having to ask the white man for everything.

RoShann shook his head free of such thoughts and led his people over every hard, rocky trail he could find, through every shallow stream of water that flowed nearby, in an effort to confuse the army's Indian scouts who would surely attempt to follow them.

12. PURSUIT

General Morgan Wells was pleased with what he saw: in fact, the sight gave him a great sense of accomplishment. He had taken on the task of rebuilding Fort Kearny without much enthusiasm, but his inspirational speeches to the troops and engineers had worked their magic. The reconstruction had progressed to near completion in just five weeks. Every available trooper had been pressed to lend a hand and the men had responded handsomely to a mixture of threats and bribery from the general himself.

He stood before the work details to address them once again:

"Men, as you know, we have been sent out here to perform a tiresome chore. It may occasionally be unpleasant, but it is worthwhile. Our brief is to contain the

Indians within their own hunting grounds, and to remove any that want to relocate to a reservation. However, make no mistake - the most important thing is that we rebuild the fort to be bigger and better than it was before!" He paused in his rhetoric momentarily to return the salute of a returning patrol, then continued:

"It is essential that the hostiles in this area should see and feel the army's presence. To the Indian, this fort represents the power and authority of the US government. So it is the duty of every man here to get off his butt and put in a good day's labour. My promise to you all is this: work hard, earn your corn, and you'll be quartered comfortably. But if you give me cause to be disappointed, I'll make sure you live to regret it!"

The general was adept at speaking to his rough, uncouth soldiers in a language they understood. The old timers moaned about the way they were being treated:

"Ain't a decent way to treat civilized folk, general!" commented an old campaigner.

"Worse'n the blacks we set free in the war!" chipped in his partner.

Ignoring the comments, the general continued: "From now on, if I'm happy with the way things are going, at the end of each day every man will receive a cupful o' whiskey…"

Hundreds of caps went flying into the air.

"For medicinal purposes only, of course. That should help to wash away the taste of the sawdust, uh? Now, get to it! Sergeant, take over here!"

"It never ceases to amaze me, general," said Colonel Darbly. "You hold a handful of oats just out of reach, and the donkey reacts!"

Wells smiled before replying tersely: "Some of those bastards would sell their own souls for a drop of gut-rot!"

Waiting patiently, the Crow Indian scouts stood outside the newly constructed doors of Fort Kearny. They were accustomed to the procedure. The Order of the Day stipulated: *'No Indian shall be allowed within the compound of Fort Kearny unless sanctioned by an officer'*.

"Sergeant! Hey, sergeant!" The sentry positioned himself to holler again, but the words died on his lips as the tough-looking first sergeant came tumbling through the doorway.

He scowled at the sentry. "You misbegotten son of a whore! You mutton-headed, addle-brained sonofabitch! Can't a man get any sleep without you standing there, yowling like some horny buffalo? Stop flapping your mouth and let those damned Indians through!" The sergeant's face was distorted with annoyance as he tucked his shirt hurriedly into his pants. Moving his belt forwards another notch, and with a final tug of his cap, he made ready to greet the new arrivals.

After a few preliminaries had been attended to the sergeant presented the Indian scouts to his platoon commander, who, after questioning them closely, made haste to the command post to deliver their report.

"Thank you, lieutenant, you may leave." General Wells returned the salute, impressed by the duty officer's efficiency. Standing in front of an expansive wall map, he looked at Colonel Darbly: "Smart young fella we have there! Let's just see what he's come up with! Mark out these positions for me, Teddy."

Colonel Darbly studied the report for a few moments, then plotted the exact coordinates of the mesa. Every day, the general had sent out survey teams with the patrols to check on the present location of each tribe and to identify their hunting boundaries.

"It's all falling into place," he commented as the colonel pinned another flag on the map with the name 'Sasquatchoni' written across it.

"Yes, sir," said the colonel, rubbing the back of his hand across his jaw, deep in thought, "but as soon as we attempt to move against them, our men will be exposed. If what the scout says is true, a few warriors concealed on top of the mesa could shoot down a regiment!"

Without taking his eyes off the Sasquatchoni marker on the wall map, Morgan Wells replied thoughtfully: "I've no reason to doubt that, Teddy." He reflected on the situation for a few moments before continuing: "Y'know, it's like some giant jigsaw puzzle. Fascinating, when all the pieces fit together."

"But what d'you make of the band o' Sasquatch heading north, general?"

"I don't know – that part of the puzzle escapes me. Where are they going, I wonder?"

"Could they be heading for the border? That's pretty wild country; only the trappers know their way around over there. And if we give chase it could cause trouble with the Hudson Bay authorities and the British."

"Maybe…" said Wells, guardedly.

He grunted, his voice suddenly hard and impatient: "Look, Teddy, let's get a hold of this campaign and get it moving. I don't like the way this damned weather is shaping up anyways. First thing in the morning I want you to head up a company and find out what the hell is going on. Take whatever supplies you'll need."

As an afterthought, the general added: "Oh, and inform O'Hara at the Indian Bureau about the Sasquatchoni movements. Do that for me, will yeh?"

PURSUIT

* * * *

RoShann was anxious to reach the mountain foothills before the army discovered his followers' whereabouts. Again and again, he exhorted his kinsmen to push themselves forward, even though some were at the point of exhaustion. At last, after a demanding trek, the group came within sight of the mountains. RoShann looked upon the mass of green pines covering the low slopes and traced their path as they soared upwards in a continuous tide. The swathe of forest rose until its progress was halted abruptly by a towering bulk of rock that seemed to hang in mid-air, looming over the lowlands in sublime grandeur.

He was careful to mask his feelings about the journey. In truth, he was afraid. The mountains formed a formidable obstacle, and he was not sure that all members of the tribe would be able to make the climb. Yet, there was no other refuge. The movements of the army had given him cause for concern. He knew that his attempts at deception had failed; heading north had not fooled the Crow scouts. Even now, they were leading the army patrol west on a trail that would eventually cut across his intended path.

Later that night, the group made camp in a thickly

wooded area. It was imperative that they obscured their path, so they lit no fires and ate only a frugal, uncooked meal. Then they pushed themselves as far into the undergrowth as they could, until they were well covered with leaves.

As night began to fall, Pancifico returned. Stooping low, the tall young warrior entered the makeshift shelter. RoShann was glad to see his most able scout.

"What did you see, Pancifico?"

The young brave replied: "Many soldiers! They are making a camp on the other side of the river - we should move. When the sun rises they will find us!"

Before answering, RoShann looked at the sprawling bodies surrounding him. They were all fast asleep. In their careless slumber, his compatriots had withdrawn from the world in a way that only the profoundly tired can do. He knew they needed some respite before continuing. Having decided upon his course of action, he turned to face the young warrior.

"Without the help of those Crow scouts, a white soldier could not find the nose on his own face!"

Pancifico smiled and nodded his head in agreement.

A crisp full moon hung low in the night sky, surrounded by an aureole of soft-blue light. Listening to the silence, RoShann and Pancifico hugged the ground closely, trying to identify the different shapes and sounds before they moved. They had travelled in a wide circle, approaching the sleeping troopers from the south. Pancifico touched RoShann's shoulder and pointed towards the huddled figures of the Crow scouts; they were sitting a short distance away from the troopers. By denying themselves the warmth of the fire, the two scouts were taking every precaution against a surprise attack - but only one seemed to be awake; he was sitting cross-legged, smoking a pipe.

Lifting their bodies carefully off the ground the Sasquatchoni warriors rubbed their cold, stiffening limbs. They had waited patiently for the slow-moving cloud to obliterate the moon; now, they had to act quickly.

RoShann gripped the neck of the sack he was carrying tightly, mindful of what it contained. Pancifico cut through the tape that secured the bundle inside, and stepped back. He watched as RoShann rotated the heavy sack above his head, before throwing it at great speed toward the string of horses. Unobserved, the two Sasquatchonis moved nearer to the Crow scouts. In the cold night air they caught the whiff of sweet tobacco smoke. The scent seemed almost to have sought them out deliberately, as it lingered around their faces before dissolving into the gloom.

Slowly, the rattlesnake emerged from the sack, angrily signaling its agitated state with its flicking tongue. Already nervous, the horses started milling around in the makeshift corral.

The young trooper on watch tried to calm them. "Whoa, whoa there! Steady boy, whoa!" Suddenly rearing, one of the terrified horses caught him unawares and he stumbled backwards, falling heavily. As he hit the ground something struck at his face, making him flinch instinctively. The light from the fire highlighted a slithering form, and he watched with wordless horror as the rattlesnake glided away. Terrified, he reached for his rifle.

"Don't shoot! Hold y'fire, yuh stupid bastard!"

The troop sergeant shouted his command again as he came to investigate the commotion. Deaf to his plea, the greenhorn trooper's mind was suddenly filled with the fear of death. He wailed: "I don't wanna die! Please help me, I don't wanna die!" He fired his rifle at the retreating reptile until his ammunition was spent. The frightened horses broke in all directions as the trooper began to cry: "Lila - help me, ma. I don't wanna die!" Clutching at his swollen face, the young man collapsed.

Fully alert now, the watchful Crow scout threw down his pipe, grabbed his rifle, and barked a guttural command at his companion.

RoShann gripped his heavy war club and sprang forward. He covered the few paces to his target very quickly and before the scout could react, swiped a vicious blow across the man's head. The Crow's skull burst open like a ripe gourd, spraying blood on the ground as he fell. Certain that the scout was dead, RoShann ran to secure the Indians' ponies. Pancifico launched himself at the other scout, his knife arm rising and falling several times before the man could defend himself.

When both Crow Indians were dead, Pancifico threw blankets over their bodies and raced to join RoShann.

Swiftly, they mounted the ponies and rode away.

The band of Sasquatchonis still encamped on top of the mesa were now engaged in a desperate struggle for survival. Their de facto leader, Mayat, was sure that the group's best hope had been to join up with their chief. He had almost managed to convince the people that there was nothing to fear from the temporary metamorphosis brought about by the herbs. If he had been allowed one more day to persuade the others to follow RoShann, he felt he might have succeeded. But the army had launched a surprise attack, bringing an end to further debate. The remnants of the tribe had not yet established any defensive positions, and some of their number were killed in the ensuing battle. Nevertheless, they had fought back ferociously and forced the troopers to retreat, leaving many dead behind.

"What will you do now, colonel?" asked O'Hara. "You've blockaded the pass, what's your next move?"

Colonel Darbly chewed the inside of his bottom lip as he stood and thought for a few moments, before replying: "I've had explicit orders from the general, Tim. If the Sasquatchoni don't surrender, I'm to bombard their position with those..." He nodded his head at the big howitzer guns.

"Yeah, but you and I both know," interrupted O'Hara, "that those guns can't be sufficiently elevated to drop a shell on the target - you're too close!"

"Sure 'nough, Tim. But I hope the noise will at least distract the Sasquatchonis' attention from the far end of the mesa - where, hopefully, I'll have a platoon of volunteers climbing the rock face. What d'you think?"

"It could work," said O'Hara, nodding his head in accord. "It might just do the job."

"I hope so, Tim. I want to be able to write in my report: *'Sasquatchoni hostilities - terminated,'* period!" He looked up at the gloomy, gray sky. "The truth is, I want to be away from here before the weather breaks. My senses are telling me to get the hell out o' here!"

"I know what you mean," said O'Hara. "It's been a while since I went a whole day without seeing or hearing a coyote. Even the prairie dogs seem to have disappeared. 'Guess they're all holed up someplace, trying to keep warm." As if to emphasize the point, a gust of wind from the plains blew a flurry of snowflakes around them.

O'Hara continued: "You know I've got to try one more time, colonel - don't you?"

Colonel Darbly stamped his feet hard on the frozen ground. "Sure you have, Tim - I understand that. But it's your neck you're sticking out, so don't stretch it too far!"

O'Hara made his way unhurriedly towards the mesa pass, taking care to ensure that both sides could see him. He picked his way through a rocky outcrop, till his horse could go no further. Leaving it tethered to a dead tree, he resumed the climb on foot. When he was halfway to the top of the promontory, he paused for a breather, glancing down at the troopers.

The impact of a bullet ricocheting off a nearby boulder jerked him back to a state of alertness: in the quiet of the late afternoon the crack of the rifle report sounded deafening.

"Why do you come again, major?" It was Mayat shouting from a concealed position higher up the crag.

O'Hara chose not to correct the comment about his rank. Instead, he lowered the white flag he was carrying and replied: "Do you always shoot at your friends!" He held up his finger and thumb with a half-inch gap between them.

Mayat left his cover and stood in full view, waiting silently, his rifle resting in the crook of his arm. He was a man for whom O'Hara had great respect.

"It has been three days since we last spoke, Mayat," said O'Hara. "I've come to speak to you again - as a friend, I hope. Y'know, this has gone on way too long. It is cold, the weather is getting worse – no one really wants to be here. Your braves and the soldiers down below are dying needlessly. You have women and children with you – they need food and shelter. They can have it. Come with me. I give you my personal guarantee that you will be treated well. Let me lead your people to the reservation!"

Marat looked at him blankly.

O'Hara continued his plea with a hint of desperation, fearing that he had no cards left to play. "I will see you get justice and…"

Mayat held up his hand and O'Hara broke off in mid-sentence. The big Sasquatchoni climbed nimbly around several boulders and scaled down the slope until he was standing directly in front of O'Hara. Frowning, he said: "I have seen the white man's justice. I saw your people hang an Indian chief in your town!" He pulled his knife from its sheath and dug at the cold red earth. Grabbing a handful of soil, he watched it trickle slowly through his fingers.

"This land was mine! But it was stolen from me. Who will give it back to me? Who will give me justice?"

There was nothing further to say. Marat and O'Hara stared at each other, unable to articulate their feelings with any greater depth. They were both aware of the other's dilemma.

Mayat turned his back and climbed up to his observation post.

Shortly after O'Hara had returned to the base camp, Colonel Darbly caught up with him.

"Too bad they turned you down, Tim. I can tell from the look on your face!" Shaking his head in despair, he shrugged his shoulders and reached for a whiskey bottle. He poured a generous shot and offered the glass to O'Hara. "Here, get that down you," he urged.

As O'Hara swallowed the drink, Darbly thrust his head outside the tent and called loudly: "Captain!"

The officer came into the canvas quarters immediately.

"Yes, sir?"

"Line up the howitzers and let's get the hell out of here!"

* * * *

RoShann lay motionless under the heavy robes and slowly opened his eyes. He was puzzled by the absence of sound. Nothing stirred; he seemed to have the world to himself. The silence worried him. There was no chattering of bird life. Pancifico should have woken him: where was he? Still, he made no effort to move.

As a comforting thought trickled into his brain, he exclaimed suddenly: "Yes, it must be!"

He threw aside the robes, a smile splitting his face. The tribe had taken shelter in an old, ramshackle stable in a deserted town. Rising quickly, he walked towards the big double doors and pushed them open. He looked about him, shielding his eyes from the unexpected snow glare. Things had changed overnight. A white blanket of fresh snowfall had transformed the view. There were no signs of life in the air, or on the ground. Everything lay dormant. The freezing draughts of cold air made him clench his teeth, and he shivered.

"Good!" he murmured, closing the doors. "The Great Spirit is with us - we are safe. No army patrol will leave the fort now!"

RoShann knew that the snowfall signified many weeks of hardship ahead for all the Indian tribes; but he was sure that, despite everything, they would survive: the strongest of their kind always did. The resourcefulness of the natural world was a source of wonder to him. All life, animal and human, was in hibernation, seemingly awed by the severity of the weather. Many creatures would be killed by the cold of winter – but others, drawing on whatever reserves of strength they could muster, would fight to live on.

After three days, the blizzard blew itself out and RoShann decided that he and his followers should leave the shelter of the stable. Outside once again, he urged his weary people - as cold and hungry as they were - to continue their journey. The elderly and the youngest sat on travois drawn behind their horses. The men rode their mounts or walked beside them through the snow, as conditions dictated. They were not yet close enough to the mountains to use the powers of the special herb, so they had to swathe themselves in whatever skins or furs they possessed to stave off the cold during the journey. In a loose, miserable procession, they waded through the deep snow.

"Look!" shouted a keen-eyed boy. "It's Pancifico!"

In the distance, they could see a dark, mounted figure against the pure-white snow. Laboriously, they trudged across the bleak landscape, made even harsher now by the bone-chilling cold. Pancifico waited for their arrival at the foot of the mountains, his horse blowing great plumes of steam from its nostrils.

RoShann approached him anxiously. "Good to see you, my friend! Have you found somewhere for us to shelter?" he asked.

"Yes!" Pancifico replied, pointing upwards through the pines. "Come!"

After an exhausting climb, the party led its horses up to the entrance of an abandoned mine. If all went well, it would be the tribe's last camp. Here, they would rest - until it was time to eat RoShann's strange medicine.

"You have done well, Pancifico," said RoShann as he gripped the young warrior's shoulder. "We must light a fire, quickly."

To the miners who had dug the shaft entrance, the site of the excavation must have seemed ideal. There was a stream of spring water running close by and the hole was concealed from casual inspection by a dense stand of pine trees. In their search for gold they had dug energetically for thirty or forty feet into the mountainside, looking for the mother lode. But, as was often the case with speculative digging, their backbreaking labour had gone unrewarded: they had broken through into a cavern that showed no evidence of gold, at all. They had, therefore, moved on to try their luck elsewhere.

Pancifico was pleased that RoShann approved of the hiding place. He had scouted many alternative locations and had explored the woods only as a last resort. Now, it was important to get a fire going; the people would feel better after some rest and a hot meal. He threw his lighted torch onto the dry woodpile and watched as the flames caught hold. Another warrior came forward and placed some dead snow hares and a turkey hen in front of the women.

"The horses, RoShann?" prompted Pancifico. He waited for his answer.

Nodding his head in acknowledgement, RoShann confirmed that the horses now presented a problem. They could not be hidden easily, and if they were left tethered outside they would betray the tribe's hideout. There was no alternative but to send them off into the wilderness. But the conclusion filled RoShann with sadness. In common with the other tribal people of the plains, the Sasquatchoni enjoyed a symbiotic relationship with creatures of the natural world; and there was no closer connection than that which existed between a warrior and his horse.

Concealing his private anguish, he said: "We have no more need of them - they must be free to run!"

RoShann brushed a light dusting of snow off the big black stallion's back. He was conscious of the futility of the exercise, but it afforded him an opportunity to touch and caress the animal, one last time. It was the horse his father had given him when he came of age.

Standing in front of the stallion he ran his fingers through its wiry mane. He murmured softly: "We have been brothers for only a short time, my friend - but now we must part. We served each other well, did we not? Manitou will care for you, as he cares for us. Live free now, Great Heart. When our lives are done, we will ride together again. Our spirits will find each other."

The animal responded by pushing its muzzle against RoShann's shoulder.

He pulled the halter off quickly and brought his lash down across the stallion's rump. Startled, the horse back-kicked and raced away.

Keeping well hidden among the spruce and cedar trees, the Crow scouts waited patiently, gripping their rifles in anticipation. Recognizing the big stallion leading the small herd, one whispered in a puzzled voice, "Sasquatchoni?"

In the short time since their arrival the cavern had acquired a snug look of permanency. The people had already taken their places around the blazing fire and were helping to prepare the food. It was not long before the mouth-watering smell of cooked meat began to tantalize their senses; they looked forward to satisfying their hunger.

Concilla watched as the young mothers caught the dripping fat and rubbed it all over the naked bodies of their children. She threw more wood onto the flames and made room for the freezing RoShann. When he was settled, she draped a heavy buffalo robe around his shoulders and tugged at his wet leggings. Making sure her hands were warm, she gently massaged his chilled limbs. As his blood circulation improved and the sensitivity slowly returned to his body, RoShann began to laugh and tried to jerk his feet away from her grasp. The infectious sound of his laughter spread to the weary people. They gathered around chuckling, and urged Concilla to render her husband helpless.

Too soon, the joy of the moment was over.

"It was good to hear you laugh again, my husband!"

Reaching out, RoShann pulled Concilla close to him. As he touched her face, they kissed tenderly. He placed his hand on her bulging belly and said: "When we reach the valley we will laugh many times together and play with our son!"

Concilla was worried. "When will we go, and how? We have no more of the magical herb."

He pulled a neatly rolled deerskin from his pouch and carefully opened the layers to expose a preserved root. Concilla studied it with a dubious expression on her face. The desiccated vegetable appeared to be totally inedible. She placed it between her teeth to test its toughness. "It has turned to stone!" she said. "But I know what to do." With that, she filled a shallow container with water and dropped the root into it. "By morning, it should be more palatable. Come, RoShann, let us eat!"

13. FREEDOM

Standing around a fire protected by a windshield the group of officers listened to Colonel Darbly. He was explaining the sequence of events that would take place the following morning.

"Well gentlemen, your comments please... Captain Craig?"

"Well sir, it's a rough plan sure 'nough, but if it helps to achieve our objective – why, colonel, I'll climb the south face of the mesa with my platoon, sir, even if it means carrying every damned trooper up there myself!"

"Very commendable, captain. But please don't strain yourself too much: I'm sure the army would like to have use of your services in years to come."

O'Hara placed a hand in front of his mouth to stifle a smile.

"Major Pierson - what d'you think?"

The short, broad, gray-haired career officer plucked at the moustache on his lip before replying: "Well, anything that brings the siege to an end before it gets really cold is a good thing as far as I'm concerned, colonel. We must take the initiative. I understand that I'm to guard the northern end of the mesa with a detachment of troopers and arrest anyone attempting to escape."

"Exactly! When I give the order for the howitzers to begin firing, make sure your men are in position. Now, gentlemen, if there are no more questions I suggest we all get our heads down. We have a long day ahead of us."

With a curt 'goodnight', the colonel dismissed the gathering.

O'Hara listened to the mournful sounds of the wind at the end of the dying autumn day and tried to rest beneath his blanket. He was full of apprehension about the action the army was pursuing and was unable to sleep. His thoughts tumbled on:

'I'm the Indian agent here. I'm supposed to represent the Indians' interests; be an intermediary; help them make deals. Not watch them get slaughtered! How has it come to this? Why won't the Sasquatchoni let me negotiate a peace for them? What can I do to prevent this?'

The questions nagged at him incessantly: but he knew it was too late to get the army to change its plans. He sighed and accepted that he would not be able to sleep. He got up and searched for his pipe, then settled himself near the fire with the blanket wound around his shoulders.

* * * *

"I'm obliged son." O'Hara grunted at the young trooper, thankful for the strong hands that grabbed him as he heaved himself onto the mesa. They had begun climbing at six a.m., just before the howitzers started firing their salvos of shot.

"Phew, that's one hell of a climb, captain!"

"I couldn't agree more, sir," said Captain Craig. He watched as O'Hara gulped down large draughts of cold morning air. The heavy boom of the howitzers had stopped.

"The shelling must have kept the Sasquatchonis occupied," said Captain Craig. "Seen nary a sight nor sound o'them. Luckily for us, they're camping at the low end of the mesa. But still, we've got to be all of six hundred feet above the surrounding terrain!"

Captain Craig looked at O'Hara for confirmation.

"Yeah," he replied, breathlessly, "it's a long way

down!"

The sergeant snapped out a quick salute and reported to the captain.

"All of the men are in position, sir. But, captain… I've seen no sign of any hostiles, as yet."

The sergeant was standing face on to the Sasquatchoni encampment, and as he finished his report his expression changed to that of a wide-eyed stare: "Well spit in my eye an' call me a liar, would y'all look at that!"

Captain Craig turned around. On the hard, sun-baked rooftops of the old adobe dwellings a gathering of Sasquatchoni had assembled.

"Thirty seven men, women and children, captain!" advised the sergeant.

"What d'you think, Mister O'Hara?" asked the captain.

"I don't rightly know, but I suggest we try to talk to them. Make sure we're showing a white flag."

When the sergeant had received the captain's order the platoon advanced slowly up the incline to where the ground leveled off.

O'Hara looked at the ancient adobe houses erected against the sheer side of the mesa, amazed at the daring ingenuity of the builders.

"Platoon – halt!" The troopers obeyed the captain's

order, but kept their rifles pointed at the tall figure of Mayat, now standing on a rooftop. From the level of the ground he seemed to loom over the soldiers like a vengeful god painted against a skyline of gray and white snow clouds.

"You come in peace with a white flag, but your soldiers carry rifles!" he boomed.

The cold northern wind had stopped blowing; there was electricity in the air, a tension in the tranquillity – like the calm before a storm. The temperature continued to fall.

Mayat held his rifle by the barrel and let it drop in front of Captain Craig. He raised his arm and ten more followed. "Our weapons are yours - without bullets, they are useless!"

Slowly, the white flag was lowered, but a fierce glare from Captain Craig quickly made the trooper hoist it aloft again. He cleared his throat and addressed Mayat:

"By direct order of the Commander of Fort Kearny, General Morgan Wells, I, Captain Henry Craig, officer of the United States Army, hereby detain you and place you under arrest. The remainder of your people will be…"

"You bloody red savage!" The words were spat out in a feral scream and followed by an explosion that made Captain Craig whirl around.

O'Hara launched himself at the young trooper just as the rifle discharged. "Hold your fire - damn you!" ordered the captain. "Hold your fire!" He rushed along the line of troopers, knocking their rifle barrels down. O'Hara and the sergeant struggled desperately to contain the aggressive trooper.

"They killed my family, shoot 'em! Those savages killed my family!"

A heavy-handed blow from the sergeant caught the enraged trooper flush on the side of his head.

"Put that soldier under close arrest, sergeant, and I mean *close!*" shouted Captain Craig in a fury.

O'Hara brushed himself down and picked up his hat. He looked at Craig.

"There's no fight left in that boy, captain – he's out."

Mayat had been wounded by the soldier's bullet, but he shrugged off the helping hands and managed to stand upright on the adobe roof once again. He shouted at the captain and his men below:

"Release the soldier! He is a warrior seeking revenge: *'blood for blood'*; in that, we are brothers!" He glanced down at the wound in his thigh, seemingly unconcerned, then continued: "For many winters gone by, our tribe covered the ground like the buffalo. When the first white man came, our chiefs made him welcome!" Mayat's accusing eyes touched lightly upon each soldier. "The white man has taken much from us: our hunting grounds; our women; our love and our innocence. What did he give in return? In return for these gifts, he gave us death!" Mayat's voice rose angrily. "Death: from a rifle barrel; at the end of a rope; by starvation - and from the sickness you call *'smallpox'!*"

The few remaining Sasquatchoni acclaimed Mayat's speech with their traditional war cries, but he silenced them with a wave of his hand.

"Tell me - who are the savages here?"

"Mayat, Mayat!" The remnants of the tribe chanted his name.

Shaking his head, Captain Craig commented: "It's going to be difficult, Mister O'Hara!"

Mayat turned his back on the soldiers and spoke rapidly to his people in their own tongue:

"You call my name with pride and praise me - but I have no great coup or victories to boast of. I am a proud warrior of the Sasquatchoni; but I am only chief here because there is no other to speak for you. You should rejoice for me, not because of my words, but because this…" he paused, looking up at the sky "…this is the day I shall die!"

Momentarily, the people held their breath, stunned by

the revelation. Mayat continued:

"Everything must die: our brother the sun; the buffalo; the blossom on the trees - and the fish in the water. Now it is time for me to die, without sadness." Mayat chose his words carefully and spoke passionately. "Together, we have prayed to 'Mother Earth'; many times we have sacrificed to her for a good harvest and for fair weather; for a good hunt against the buffalo; or for fish to return to our streams. But now, She has sent us a sign. We have nothing left: no homes, no land, and no freedom. It is the end, my friends! There is no more She can do for us: it is time to return to Her bosom, to become one with the Earth again! She gave me life, and will welcome me with open arms – then, She will send my soul onwards to ride with Manitou, the Great Spirit!"

The others listened in a subdued mood, suddenly filled with a terrible despondency. They were hypnotized by his words, as he continued:

"I was born into this tribe as an innocent child; but, due to the teachings of our elders and the example of our fiercest braves, I grew up to be a proud, strong man. Thanks to them, and to you, I will leave this life with something of the highest value, worth more than any bauble treasured by the white men. Something that can never be taken from me, because it lives within me: the dignity of a Sasquatchoni warrior!"

Though O'Hara had never mastered the Sasquatchoni language, he could understand some of the more commonly used words. As he listened to Marat an uncomfortable feeling descended on him; a premonition, perhaps, that something dramatic was about to take place. There was little to distract him from his gloom, and his unease persisted. He wondered if it was just the cold gray sky that had set his backbone shivering. From the company's elevated position on top of the mesa the plains below were spread out in all their bleak austerity.

Mayat picked up his bow and a quiver full of arrows. The troopers - wary and restless - started to lift their rifles.

"Steady men, hold your fire!" cautioned Captain Craig.

Mayat turned around to face the soldiers. He stood, oblivious to the cold, in his breechclout, a blanket hanging from his shoulders like a cloak. Then he raised his lance high above his head, and threw the weapon into the frozen ground in front of the troopers.

"Hoka Hey!" The words were drawn out and then cut dead, but seemed to linger in the chill morning air.

O'Hara moved forward quickly, protesting: "Mayat, no!"

Ignoring his plea, the giant Sasquatchoni turned and

ran across the flat rooftops of the adobe houses, repeatedly shouting the strange call, before hurling himself into space.

O'Hara watched, powerless to act, as Mayat appeared to hover in the air for several seconds. Then he was gone.

It was the older Sasquatchoni people who responded first; they realized that Mayat had articulated an unspoken truth. Their lives were filled with humiliation and anguish and there was no reason to continue. They knew, as well as he, that the sacred 'Mother Earth' would welcome them. The spectacle of Mayat's death and his strong personality drew them on. An old woman was the first to go over the edge, swiftly followed by several mothers clutching their infant children; then, the remaining husbands and wives.

'Hoka Hey' echoed again and again until the adobe rooftop was empty.

O'Hara blinked his eyes in disbelief.

"Stop! Stop damn you!" Although the protest was futile, Captain Craig called out again. Shaking his head he stared at the vacant space. "It's madness!" he said, his voice trailing away.

An updraught of wind from the plains hit the mesa, howling and moaning its way through the silent adobes. Big flakes of snow started falling heavily.

"Tell me something, Mister O'Hara," said Captain Craig. "*Hoka Hey*'. What does it mean?"

O'Hara gave him a long, sideways look before replying: "*It's a good day to die*'."

14. STRANGE MEDICINE

The small herd of white-tailed wapiti moved slowly through the snow-bound clearing. Suddenly, the leader of the group stopped, its ears alert. It raised its head high in an attempt to locate and identify an elusive scent, its delicate nostrils twitching rapidly. With one leg poised, it held its ground, unsure whether to run or to stay in its position; the others, standing perfectly still like fossilized trees in a petrified forest, waited upon the lead buck's decision. Finally, the large male began to graze again, and the others took their cue to lower their heads and continue foraging. It was at that moment that a heavy war arrow struck a doe just behind its shoulder.

The 'thunk' of the arrow as it made contact with the doe's yielding flesh broke the fragile tranquillity of the scene. Sensitive to any strange sound, the rest of the deer bounded away. The wounded animal made frantic efforts to follow the herd, but it collapsed and died after just a few strides.

The only sound was the occasional rustle amongst the pines as a snow-bowed branch abruptly shook off its burden, sending a powdery white cascade crashing to the ground.

Pancifico congratulated himself: he had no need to endure the bitter cold any longer. He eased his muscular frame down from the tree and rubbed and slapped at his frozen limbs. His patience had been rewarded. "Today, my people will eat well!"

Concilla had been hurt by RoShann's words. He had ordered her to stay behind, even though there was enough of the strange root for both of them. Resentful and angry, she gritted her teeth as she held her knife high, before plunging it forcefully into the carcass. She pulled down viciously with both hands and watched as the deer's intestines spilled out, covering the floor. Running her fingers through the innards, she and the other women picked out little delicacies; no part of the body would be wasted.

"RoShann had to go alone," she declared aloud. "He has much wisdom!" Her anger forgotten, she helped the other squaws with the skinning.

SASQUATCH MAN

* * * *

General Morgan Wells raised his glass. "Gentlemen, a toast! To the officers and men of Fort Kearny who fell during the recent campaign!" The small band of officers swallowed their brandies respectfully, then waited for the general to continue.

"Washington is pleased, and I'm personally very satisfied with the way the exercise was carried out. And, as a result of it, the Sasquatchoni Indians will cause no further trouble to anyone. There were some regrettable deaths on both sides – but that's just the fortunes of war. Of course, those words are for public consumption, you understand... If I may lapse back into army language for a moment - the Sasquatchoni screwed it up; they played a poor hand. And we can be thankful for that!"

He picked out a sheaf of paper from the pile in front of him. "The eastern news sheets are having a field day. Quote: *'U.S. cavalry charge drives last Sasquatchoni Indians over cliff edge – hundreds die!'* Here's another: *'In barbaric act of retribution U.S. troopers throw Indian prisoners off mountain top.'*"

He crushed the report into a ball and threw it over his shoulder. "It seems as long as their circulation keeps on climbing, those editors will print anything, even downright lies!" He tapped the remaining papers with a stiff forefinger. "The very same papers report nothing of the Sioux or Cheyenne, who have taken refuge in the Canadas - or of the other tribes who have voluntarily sought shelter on the reservations! We owe that particular success to our Indian Agent, Mister Tim O'Hara." Murmuring their approval, the company lifted their glasses to O'Hara. He said nothing in reply, but returned the general's gaze with a studied expression on his face.

"Most of us have our wives and families here, in Fort Kearny," continued the general, "and winter is fast taking hold. That means our operational patrols will have to be curtailed. The best we can do now, is bed down and maintain a minimal presence in the surrounding area. We'll resume normal activities in the spring." Refilling his glass the general paused. "Oh yeah, before I forget! Our scouts have reported some Indians holding out near 'Snow Mountain' – I believe that's what the tribes call it, at any rate. In the morning, therefore, Colonel Darbly will select a patrol to investigate." The general looked at O'Hara. "And you're invited to the party, as well."

O'Hara could barely suppress a smile. "You've been reading my mind, general. I'm obliged."

"Never play poker with him, Tim!" chipped in Colonel Darbly. "I did - he won the shirt off my back, and to add to my embarrassment he wouldn't lend me a blanket to cover my shame…'

"The truth is, Timmo, we never had a blanket big 'nough to cover his shame!" laughed the general.

The ribald comments and the contagious laughter bounced from one man to another. After the meal, coffee was served and the cigar box passed around. Then it was time for the company to disperse.

General Wells walked with O'Hara as they made their way back to their quarters. "D'you think it could be the Sasquatchonis holed up there on the mountain, Tim? We never did account for all of 'em."

"Could be, general. There was a group seen heading in that direction."

The general started patting the pockets of his coat absentmindedly. "Oh, by the way… I found this in the washroom… it just has to be yours."

He retrieved the object from his coat pocket and dropped it into O'Hara's outstretched hand. It was a heavy gold signet ring

O'Hara smiled in recognition. "Ah… that's right, I took it off when I was shaving. How did you know it was mine?"

Laughing, the general replied: "Who else, but a sentimental Irishman named Tim, would have a ring engraved with a shamrock and the letter 'T'?"

It had taken RoShann two days of hard tracking to reach the hidden valley and to return with a supply of the magical herb. He hoped he had enough, and that all of his people would use it.

Concilla was the first to greet him, as usual. In great excitement, she asked after her family, eager for news.

"The spirits have blessed your sister, Neli, with another child – a boy. Red Horse is in good health. He and the children wait to welcome us all!" He paused to swallow the last of the hot, berry-flavoured drink Concilla had given him. "The valley is still warm and green; as beautiful as it ever was: there, we shall find peace!"

"RoShann! RoShann!" A warrior stumbled into the cavern, his shoulders heaving with exhaustion.

"What is it Pancifico?"

Pancifico managed to gasp out his warning: "Soldiers! Soldiers have entered the forest; they are coming this way!"

A wave of fear and consternation swept though the group. They were tired and had only a few rifles with which to fend off an attack.

Holding up his hand, RoShann managed to calm his people. "We have enough time – remember, the snow is our friend."

He beckoned to Pancifico. "Come, a new life awaits us!"

Each member of the group now consumed their own share of the root, still with some trepidation. An old warrior examined his portion suspiciously. He waved his hand around the seated circle and said: "I am old enough to remember the women giving birth to each one of you! I have seen many winters; but never have I seen such a strange herb!" He held it to his nose and sniffed at it speculatively.

"Eat!" urged RoShann as he backtracked along the forest path. "There is no more time to talk. Eat the herb and you will have a chance to survive!"

Encouraged by Concilla, the whole group began chewing on the root. Some pulled faces at the bitter taste of the plant. It dried up their mouths, and they found it necessary to wash the pulp down with sips of water.

Looking at each other with apprehension, they nervously inspected their bodies for any signs of change to their appearance. It took a few moments for their digestive systems to break down the root fibers, and for their blood to absorb the potent chemicals. Some of the group sat perfectly still, unable to move, whilst others walked around until they collapsed. Some stamped their feet as a numb sensation began to spread throughout their bodies. People began to realize that they were powerless to prevent the transfiguration from occurring; whatever was going to happen could not be stopped by anyone, and the knowledge was frightening. As they tried to control their fears their tightly drawn facial muscles twitched and jerked; their nostrils flared in panic and their eyes moved wildly.

But the terror was transitory: it receded as their breathing became easier, and they experienced a warm sensation returning to their limbs. Their leg muscles tingled and started to contract. The temperature of their bodies began to increase as they responded to the drug; a sheen of perspiration glistened on their foreheads. The self-generated warmth made them feel uncomfortable and they felt compelled to shed their clothing in an attempt to cool down.

As they threw off their clothing they realized that their bodies were becoming those of giants. Their enlarged pectoral muscles jumped and bounced as they flexed their arms. Their minds reeled with the weirdness of the transformation and the horror of what they had become: unconscious emotions gnawed at them; they wanted the changes to stop: to be over. Gradually, fine, reddish-brown hair began to sprout from the pores of their skin until their entire bodies were covered with a thick, matted growth of pungent fur.

RoShann came running back to them. "You must hurry; the soldiers are near! I will stay to cover our tracks. Now, go - all of you! Run!"

Gathering outside the mine entrance, they waited for Concilla to join them. In the daylight the people were able to examine each other more closely and were startled by the feral appearance they had all acquired. They began to feel exhilarated; they looked formidable. They had become enormous animals, the fearsome beasts of some tribal legend: they looked wilder than any demon conjured up by a shaman's trance.

"No! We must go together!" Concilla's voice was raised in stringent protest. "We will wait for you!"

"It is too late to change our plan," said RoShann. "I have asked Pancifico to keep watch. He and I will join you later. You must lead the others to the valley, Concilla. Do not fail them. Go now!"

Reluctantly, Concilla obeyed his command and stood with the main party, doing her best to hide her fears. All were ready and eager to begin the final journey. Making sure their packs were secure and without looking back, they followed Concilla upwards, seeking cover amongst the pine trees.

STRANGE MEDICINE

Reveling in their new guise, the remnants of the tribe climbed higher and higher, enjoying the physical effort it required. For the first time in many days and weeks, they were full of hope.

RoShann had spoken the truth: his medicine was strong. Keeping close to each other the small group disappeared into the mist surrounding the rugged uplands of Snow Mountain.

* * * *

Lieutenant Clayton Poliakoff was pleased to have been selected by Colonel Darbly to lead the Sasquatchoni search detail. It was his first command as a junior officer. 'Polly', as the men universally referred to him, was being blooded under the watchful eyes of General Wells, and he knew that much was expected of him. The sergeant accompanying the detail was an experienced soldier and Polly had decided to listen to his advice before making any moves. The mission might otherwise end in disaster - and he did not want to disappoint anybody, or ruin his budding career.

The icy wind and rain had continued all morning and even on horseback the members of the company found it difficult to keep their boots dry. Riding at the head of the column, Poliakoff realized the sergeant was showing signs of increasing frustration at their slow progress, so he ordered him to speak his mind.

The sergeant said in a respectful, but somewhat jaded manner: "Lieutenant – from the look of them clouds ahead and the feel of the wind we're gonna be riding through a snowstorm soon enough. It's getting real cold and the men are suffering quite a bit. The way things are going, I reckon we'll all end up frozen to death if we don't get around a fire before the light fades. May I suggest, sir, that if we find no sign of Indians in the next hour, we head back and dry out at the relay station?"

Grabbing at his kerchief to stifle a sneeze, Poliakoff replied, hesitantly: "Very well, sergeant - I'm inclined to agree. That might be the best course."

"Now, just hold it right there," interrupted O'Hara as he held his horse alongside.

"What is it, sir?"

O'Hara pulled his mount around hard and looked at Poliakoff. He spoke softly, but with a stony-faced gaze that would brook no argument. "I'm going on to the old prospectors' diggings, lieutenant - with or without you and the rest of the company. The general wants us to make contact with the Indians at Snow Mountain and bring them in. This may be our last chance and I'm not going to see it thrown away, just so I can warm my ass by the nearest fire. When I write my official report for the general I want to be able to say we tried everything - not that we gave up because of the weather! You want to make your mark, lieutenant? Then follow the general's order and get the job done. Or maybe you don't mind having your balls torn off by the general when we get back?"

Without waiting for a reply, O'Hara spurred his horse and pushed ahead.

Poliakoff swallowed hard and blinked the rain from his eyes before shouting: "Sergeant! Get the men in line, we're going on!"

"Yes, lieutenant," replied the disappointed sergeant. He turned to vent his wrath on the hapless troopers. "Alright now, stop bellyaching! Move yourselves, you whiskey-sodden, pox-riddled saddle tramps. Get those mule-headed donkeys you call horses out of here…"

* * * *

Having concealed himself amongst some dark evergreen shrubs, Pancifico watched the column of troopers slowly advancing towards its objective. He was thankful for the transformation brought about by the herbs; the reddish brown color of his thick hair blended well with the late autumn backdrop, providing a perfect camouflage. He was determined to assist his tribe in whatever way he could. Though he had been asked simply to watch the movements of the troopers, it was obvious to him that more would be required; the white men were closing in. It was now vital that he should create a diversion to give RoShann and the others a chance of escaping capture.

He lifted his rifle and adjusted the sight carefully, pulling the butt well into his shoulder. His forefinger curled around the trigger, gently increasing its pressure. The ambush was set...

"I wish young Polly boy had listened t'yuh, sergeant," said a trooper with a soft southern drawl. "We'd have bin at the relay station drying off b'now, I reckon."

"Never you mind, boy - another hour and we'll be finished."

The bullet hit the sergeant smack in middle of his temple; then an explosive sound shattered the brittle silence, echoing and rebounding across the mountain. Alarmed by the sudden disturbance a flock of wild geese lifted into the air, calling clamorously to each other as they fled south. Throwing themselves into the deep snow, the troopers waited breathlessly. Poliakoff and O'Hara came running back to their position.

"Over here, lieutenant!" called a trooper kneeling beside the fallen sergeant.

"Timmo!" shouted another.

O'Hara looked around to find a face that suited the voice; he settled on an old veteran he had known from years back. "Hi, Murph! What's happening?"

"The sergeant's dead, Timmo – all we can do is worry about the living. It's just like old times, ain't it?"

"Yeah, that's right, you old bastard," said O'Hara affectionately. "You were the best first sergeant I ever bad – till you got yourself pissed and planted one on the colonel's chin. You sure bollixed that one up, Murph! I didn't know you were on this ride – I'll bet you're glad you came…"

Murphy shrugged his shoulders. "'Tis me last chance, Tim!" He nodded towards the corpse. "Those sergeant tags are mine! But if I tells young Polly what me eyes have seen - why, he'll slap a court martial on me for being drunk. That boy's stupid, but keen as hell, and as God's me judge, me poor lips haven't had as much as a tipple o' the hard stuff!" Murphy sent a hasty glance upwards and blessed himself quickly.

"What are you talking about?" said O'Hara, irritably. "What did you see?"

"That cluster of trees on your left: that's where the shot came from. But I saw something else... I saw a big, hairy beastie running for cover!" He blurted the words out quickly, like a child fearing chastisement.

"C'mon Murphy... it's gotta be some grizzly bear." O'Hara's tone was full of disdain.

"Oh, I'm sure it was, lad, that's what I'm thinking. But... how could a bear carry a rifle?"

"Gimme fifteen minutes. I'll try to get 'round the side and see if we can flush him out. Inform the lieutenant and send in a couple o'shots."

Ignoring his civilian status O'Hara took over command. Using the deep snow and every bit of available cover, he rested near the position that Murphy had indicated. His warm breath lingered like steam in the freezing morning air, so he pulled a kerchief over his mouth to contain it. He let his eyes probe every possible hiding place beneath the trees and settled on a thick bank of dull-green honeysuckle, sprinkled with snow. A sudden fusillade of rifle fire made him bury his face in a drift.

'Those cross-eyed bastards are shooting at me!'

He listened as bullets struck the boughs of the cottonwood trees above his head. With relief, he heard someone give the cease-fire command; but his attention remained locked on the honeysuckle: there was something thrashing about in the bush.

'I bet it's some goddamn mountain man gone loco!' he thought.

He caught a momentary glimpse of a large figure behind the bushes. It started to run away, darting through the thick cover, moving up the slope. O'Hara gripped his revolver and followed the crimson bloodstains on the snow. He was not entirely sure what - or who - he was tracking. He ran for some distance, then stopped, puzzled. He stared hard at the huge, impressed footprints. *'Only a madman would tramp around out here with no boots on!'* His eyes focused on the dense undergrowth where the tracks ended - then opened wide with astonishment at the sight of the tall, red-haired beast that suddenly emerged to confront him.

Its appearance was so unexpected, so dramatic, that the spectacle momentarily fazed O'Hara; his mind went completely blank with shock and surprise.

"Wha' - What in God's name...?" His voice was a whisper. The monstrous being was bleeding badly from a gaping wound in its side. O'Hara was transfixed. Slowly, the ape-like creature raised its rifle, though it did not fire the weapon. Whether it was unable, or unwilling to do so, O'Hara could not tell.

With his nerves poised in taut awareness, he reacted

instinctively. He fired a single bullet from his own gun. The huge beast's body convulsed with the impact of the round and it fell down, still clutching its rifle. O'Hara had a chance to finish it off immediately, but he could not bring himself to deliver the *'coup de grâce'*. Instead, he lowered his gun arm and watched in fascination. The creature was still a threat: O'Hara held his breath as it continued to point its rifle at him. Slowly, the barrel dipped. The shaggy head drooped onto its chest; the beast man's will to live was fast seeping away. Then it pitched forward like some giant redwood tree sawn though at the base and tumbled down the incline, before coming to rest abruptly against a lichen-covered boulder.

Holstering his gun, O'Hara approached the body warily, as if in a dream. Filled with curiosity, he turned the corpse over until it lay flat on its back. He knelt to examine the body and a wave of sadness swept over him; for some indefinable reason he began to regret the killing. It made no sense, but there was something about the creature's eyes that made it look almost human; like someone he had once met, but could no longer quite recognize. Certainly, this was no bear...

Backing off, he pondered the uncomfortable emotions the creature's appearance had sparked in him. *'What's the matter with me? It's just some kind of ape – that's all!'*

Shaking his head, he heard Murphy and the lieutenant calling him. He responded with a wave of his arm. As the coldness began to bite through his thick clothing, O'Hara glanced at the corpse one last time. But something had changed… the body looked different. He examined it more closely and gave a start of stunned amazement as he realized what had occurred whilst his back had been turned. He rubbed his eyes. Patches of reddish-brown hair from the beast man's body had started to blow away on the frosty mountain breeze, exposing areas of tan-colored skin. A weird re-formation of its features was rapidly taking effect. The muscles were bubbling up from within and then subsiding, shrinking in size until, at last, they had melded into the smooth flesh of a well-built Sasquatchoni warrior. And the face being gradually revealed was, indeed, one he had seen before…

'What the hell!' O'Hara began to fear he was suffering from some form of snow madness. He had heard mountain men tell stories of strange apparitions they had seen beyond the snow line, when the cold had weakened their spirits and muddled their heads. *'No! Dammit, no!'* He would not let it happen to him… Grabbing a handful of snow he rubbed it savagely over face and head. Bewildered, he looked again at the primeval forest and the thin mountain mist that was creeping closer. The trees

seemed to be crowding in on him, enveloping him; which way was up? Or down? Nothing moved. Not a single bird cry broke the deafening silence. The hackle hairs on the back of his neck began to rise. He had always prided himself on his ability to stay composed in difficult situations, but for the first time in his life he experienced a raw fear of the unknown. He was scared.

He tried to rationalize the encounter, but could come up with no satisfactory conclusion and shook his head in frustration.

"Hey, Tim lad!" The warm voice of Murphy broke through to him. "Did we get the bastard?"

"Yeah, we got him," said O'Hara, flatly. "I sure could use a swig of whiskey, Murph."

"Never so much as a piddling drop touches me lips these days, Tim lad! I'm a changed man!"

"Just gimme the bottle, for Chrissake!" yelled O'Hara. His voice was so hoarse and unsteady that Murphy immediately understood his friend was in no mood for joshing. Without further ado, he reached into his hip pocket and handed over the half-bottle he always carried with him for 'medicinal purposes'.

Murphy watched anxiously as mouthfuls of the fiery liquor disappeared down O'Hara's throat.

"Was it the big hairy fella, Tim?"

O'Hara paused to rub the back of his hand across his mouth before replying: "Just a trick o'the light, Murph. That's all it was - just a trick o'the light!"

15. SASQUATCH MAN

The column advanced unchallenged until it reached the copse of trees screening the deserted gold mine. Lieutenant Poliakoff issued his orders without removing his eyes from the snow-dusted ferns and thorny shrubs beneath the trees. "Sergeant Murphy, fire a warning shot and run up a white flag. If our scouts are correct, this is where the Sasquatchoni are hiding. And remember: our job here is to escort these people to a reservation, not to shoot them!"

The soldiers soon discovered the entrance to the mine, but no Indian warrior appeared to oppose them.

"We'd better check it out, lieutenant," said Murphy.

"Yes, I guess we better had. Take your pick of the men, sergeant. Search the mine and then let's get out of here."

"If you would allow me, lieutenant," interjected

O'Hara. He chose his words carefully: "I know the chief of this tribe... well, I've met him a few times. I'd like to join the search party. If the Indians are in there, they're more likely to respond to me than anyone else."

Cold, wet and hungry, Poliakoff hesitated, uncertain of his ground. But the hard look on O'Hara's face made it plain he would not be deterred.

"Sergeant Murphy! Select a couple of men to accompany Mister O'Hara."

"Oakes and Webb - you'll do!" bellowed Murphy, enjoying his elevation in rank. The two men stood side by side as Murphy walked over to them. He continued quietly: "Now listen, fellas: watch his back for me, will yuh? I owe him!"

The other troopers huddled under their cloaks and looked on disinterestedly as the three men struggled through the snow to the mine entrance.

Trying hard to stop his teeth from chattering, Poliakoff said: "Murphy, this place makes me feel as though we're the only people left alive in the whole goddam world."

"I was thinking the very same thing m'self, lieutenant; if there ever were any Indians here, they're long gone b'now!" He handed his half-bottle of whiskey to the lieutenant.

"When they return, Murphy, we're going back to the relay station."

O'Hara stopped just inside the mine entrance and motioned to the troopers to stand guard. He knotted his kerchief around the barrel of his rifle to form a wad. With luck, he figured it would give him sufficient light for a couple of minutes.

"RoShann! Anyone there?"

There was only the black silence. With the blaze from the smouldering kerchief lighting his way, he stumbled into the passage.

The two troopers watched as O'Hara went further inside the mineshaft.

"D'you really think there's any chance of Indians being back there, Oakesy?"

"No chance!"

"But shouldn't we have our rifles ready, just in case?"

"Nope, you take my word on it, Webb, we'd have heard something before now. Besides, I've got my own worries. My guts are killing me!" Oakes patted his paunch.

"You've got more flesh there than a pregnant buffalo," jibed Webb

"I gotta take a leak!" Oakes started unbuttoning the

front of his pants. "It's the wonder of mankind, Webb; yuh takes it in one end and yuh squeezes it out t'other!"

He stood with his legs astride, waiting expectantly; but nothing happened. "Say Webb! Yuh don't think my water's frozen, huh?"

Webb countered laconically: "No such luck - I reckon it's your brains!"

"It's too dang cold, that's what it is," said Oakes. "What I want is one of those gals from Jacques Fleur's saloon. That'd warm me up. Bet yuh I could go a skinful then!"

"Oakesy, you're a dirty old bastard, you know that! What the hell would you do if one of those big Sasquatch came running through here, huh?"

With a mischievous look on his face, Oakes retorted: "I'd piss right in his eye! Yuh wouldn't know this, Webb, being an easterner an' all that, but Indians don't like salt water - and that's the truth!"

"Pshaw! Oakesy, you wouldn't recognize the truth if you tripped over it in broad daylight!" Webb's jabbing finger emphasized the point.

"Smart ass!" murmured Oakes. Grinning broadly, he leaned back and sent a stream of urine arching through the air.

O'Hara's makeshift torch guttered out leaving the corridor blacker than ever. He edged forward blindly, remarking under his breath: "I hope there's no more passage ways branching off out o' here... or you could be in trouble, old man."

It was with no small feeling of relief that he caught the unmistakable scent of an encampment nearby.

"RoShann?" He was standing at the entrance to the cavern located at the back of the mine. For a brief moment a fire flared up within it, casting a huge shadow on the far wall. O'Hara could not identify the figure he saw; it appeared to be swathed in an old buffalo robe

"Major!"

"RoShann! Is that you?" He moved closer to the figure and held a finger across his mouth to indicate that RoShann should speak only in whispers.

O'Hara watched the troopers relieving themselves with an amused look on his face. He cleared his throat and said: "Lucky for you there's no wind blowing through this passage way, Oakesy!"

"Ha, whoops!" the startled trooper exclaimed. "Yuh sure 'nough knows how to scare the shit out o' abody, Mister O'Hara!"

Oakes finished tucking in his shirt and buttoning

down his pants, then enquired cheerily: "No Indians?"

"That's right, Oaksey," said O'Hara. "I've been all the way down to the far end – nothing. They're gone."

"Well, the sooner we gets to that relay station, Webb, the sooner yuh can buy that bottle a' whiskey yuh owe me. C'mon!"

Oakes walked out of the mine with the luckless Webb following.

O'Hara watched the troopers slipping and sliding down the snow-covered slope. When they had reached ground level, he yelled after them: "I'm gonna scout around a bit longer. Tell the lieutenant I'll catch up!" With a final acknowledgement from Poliakoff, the column turned and began its journey to the relay station.

With some difficulty, O'Hara made his way back to the cavern. When he arrived, he found that RoShann had rebuilt the fire. He was sitting in the shadows on the far side of the flames, wrapped in a thick buffalo hide.

O'Hara sat close to the fire with a discarded blanket around his shoulders and watched the steam rise from his wet boots. "It's been a long time," he said.

"Yes, major. Many people have died since we last met – and a few have gained glory by their deeds."

O'Hara briefly related the story of Mayat's death and

the catastrophic aftermath for the remnants of the Sasquatchoni tribe. RoShann simply chewed on a root as he listened, lost in thought. O'Hara could not see him clearly, nor judge the effect his words were having on him.

Shaking his head sadly, he finished his tale. "All of the others followed Mayat. One by one, they jumped off the mesa. They are all dead..."

"A man is in charge of his own life; it is his to dispose of in any way that pleases him," said RoShann bluntly. "I do not grieve for them, major; they ride with Manitou now. Though our separation is a cause for sorrow, we will not be apart forever. When it is my time to die, I will do so with a smile on my face, because then I will join the ranks of the dead, and we will hunt together once more."

RoShann reached down at his side, searching for something. He found the object and laid it across his knee, then carefully removed its covering of soft-cured deerskin. His most treasured possession was gradually revealed: Tonala's smoking pipe. He filled the bowl with tobacco flakes and passed it over to O'Hara.

Taking a smouldering sprig from the fire the major drew deeply on the pleasant tasting smoke and reminisced about the past. "I have smoked this pipe many times with your father," he said appreciatively. "It is a beautiful thing."

"It has often consoled me, when I needed to remain calm," said RoShann.

O'Hara looked at the pipe in the glow from the fire. The warm light shone obliquely across its angular form and glanced off the polished metal surfaces. With infinite care, an unknown Indian craftsman had carved figures of men and animals on the bowl, and inlaid the stem with gold and silver tracery.

Passing the pipe back to RoShann, O'Hara told him of Pancifico's death and of the mysterious transformation that had occurred to his body. As he spoke, he felt embarrassed at the thought that he was squandering RoShann's respect for him; surely, no sane man could believe such a tale...

"Well that's what happened, RoShann," he said. "It's kinda hard for me to tell you about all this. But... I know what I saw. I'm sorry about the death of your warrior. I would not have shot him if I had known who it was. But he had me scared - I'd be a liar if I didn't admit it." He stared silently into the depths of the fire.

RoShann passed the pipe back to him. As he did so, the hide covering his shoulders fell away to reveal a hand and forearm covered with thick, reddish-brown hair.

O'Hara froze, his mouth agape.

Observing the look of incomprehension on his face,

RoShann said: "Do not be alarmed, my friend." He threw off the heavy buffalo robe and moved out of the shadows.

O'Hara backed off a few paces and gaped speechlessly at RoShann's body, now completely covered in hair. His size was overwhelming, and he had the appearance of a brutish animal.

"You are the only white man I ever trusted, major," said RoShann. "Always, your words were full of strength. But is your mind strong enough to contain this secret?"

O'Hara gasped: "Who... who would believe me, if I spoke about it!" There were a hundred things he wanted to ask at that moment, but he restrained himself and listened as the young chieftain ignored the irony of his words.

"Let your eyes feast well, major. I am the last Sasquatchoni warrior you will ever see. When we part, the Sasquatchoni nation will disappear - like the buffalo, which went before us. With the passing of the seasons we will be forgotten. That is as it should be." He made a scissor movement with his hands.

O'Hara's confused mind could stay silent no longer. He threw questions at RoShann, pleading for a rational explanation. "But how? Why? Where are the rest of your people? What makes your body change like this? How d'you do it? Please tell me..."

RoShann told of his hunting trip in search of the

eagle's feathers and of the strange events that had followed.

"My people and I will go to the valley and live life as we once did - before the white man entered these lands. You must never look for the valley, major; its location must remain a secret."

"I give you my word, RoShann."

O'Hara watched, hypnotized, as the metamorphosis of RoShann's body reached its finale and the change was complete. His friend was barely recognizable. He looked away, seeking the reassurance of a familiar sight; he could see RoShann's discarded clothing scattered around the fire, along with some cooking pots, rifles and a few other implements that made life bearable for the prairie Indians.

At that moment, his mind could not assimilate what it had witnessed. As a former soldier and frontiersman O'Hara had always followed the old maxim: *'Believe nothing, till you've seen it with your own eyes'* - but this was too much. Shaking his head, he covered his eyes and rubbed at them gently, trying to ease the tiredness away. His senses rebelled at having to accept what he had seen; but there was no other path. Unconsciously, he scratched at the stubble on his cheek and tried to control his racing heart.

"It is late, major. I must go; my people are waiting for me."

Standing outside the mine's entrance O'Hara shivered as the cold wind bit into him. RoShann's tawny fur seemed to merge naturally into the dun colors of the surrounding willows, cottonwoods and pine.

Although the Sasquatchoni's body was now that of an intimidating monster, his dark-rimmed eyes remained familiar and friendly. O'Hara looked up at him: a tide of unvoiced thoughts surged between them; regrets, apologies, questions and justifications: but there was no time for anything else to be discussed.

RoShann offered his smoking pipe to O'Hara as a parting gift. Searching hastily though his pockets, the major gave his gold signet ring to RoShann. "Here -" he said, "remember me from time to time. It's got my initial on it."

RoShann smiled as he squeezed the ring onto the tip of his smallest finger.

The snow was falling now in large, moth-like flakes and a belt of thick, gray cloud obscured the sun. Soon, the skies would be flushed with pink and the temperature would fall even further: there was a long, cold night ahead. Neither man spoke a word; it was enough to share the silence.

RoShann's giant hand gripped the major's forearm in a gesture of farewell - and with that, he started his climb upwards through the freezing mist. His reddish-brown fur quickly became flecked with snow as he ploughed on, leaving a long trail of oversized footprints behind.

O'Hara watched him for a while, pleased that the last of the Sasquatchoni would escape; as he did so, he felt a growing sense of unreality creeping over him. His mind raced with the implications of the tale he had been told… Any tracks left by RoShann would soon be obliterated by fresh snowfall, and there were no other witnesses to the scene.

He glanced away, momentarily, to check that his horse was still securely tethered. Reassured, he looked back at the rocky slopes, but could no longer see RoShann. The tall figure of the Sasquatchoni warrior had become one with the mountain.

O'Hara turned to leave as the sun sank behind the highest peaks and the hillside was thrown into shadow.

High above, an eagle soared on the wind and swooped away.

ABOUT THE AUTHOR

John P. Burling has been writing poetry and novels for 25 years, inspired by the work of Paul Verlaine, E. E. Cummings and Jack London. His interests include Wild West cinematography; the history of Hawaii; classical and modern music; and, as a young man, the noble art of boxing. He grew up in East London during the Blitz and after a period of National Service spent his entire working life in the City. He is now retired and devotes himself to writing, painting and traveling. He lives in Essex with his wife, Val.

Printed in Great Britain
by Amazon.co.uk, Ltd.,
Marston Gate.